THE LOST DIARY

The Lost Diary

Julie White

sononis
PRESS

WINLAW, BRITISH COLUMBIA

Copyright © 2014 by Julie White

Cover artwork copyright © 2014 by Joan Larson

Library and Archives Canada Cataloguing in Publication

White, Julie, 1958–, author
    The lost diary / Julie White.

Issued in print and electronic formats.

ISBN 978-1-55039-234-0 (pbk.).—ISBN 978-1-55039-236-4 (ebook)
    I. Title.
PS8645.H54L67 2014   jc813'.6   C2014-906026-2   C2014-906027-0

Sono Nis Press most gratefully acknowledges support for our publishing program provided by the Government of Canada through the Canada Book Fund and the Canada Council for the Arts, and by the Province of British Columbia through the British Columbia Arts Council and the Book Publishing Tax Credit, Ministry of Provincial Revenue.

Edited by Laura Peetoom
Copy edited by Audrey McClellan
Proofread by Dawn Loewen
Cover and interior design by Frances Hunter
Cover and frontispiece art by Joan Larson
Author photo by Andrea Blair, Paper Horse Photography

Published by	Distributed in the U.S. by
Sono Nis Press	Orca Book Publishers
Box 160	Box 468
Winlaw, BC V0G 2J0	Custer, WA 98240-0468
1-800-370-5228	1-800-210-5277

books@sononis.com
www.sononis.com

The Canada Council | Le Conseil des Arts
for the Arts | du Canada

Printed and bound in Canada by Houghton Boston Printing.

Printed on acid-free paper that is forest friendly (100% post-consumer recycled paper) and has been processed chlorine free.

To my father, who was always ready
for any new adventure

....

Many thanks to Pam Arthur and Robin Hahn
for so generously sharing their experiences in
international equestrian competition.

1

Something was tickling her ear.

Faye pulled the bedcovers up over her head, blocking out the light. The tickling moved to her hand, first the knuckles and now the tender, thin skin between her fingers. Shuddering, she sat up and glared at the culprit.

"Stubby! How did you get up on my bed?"

The old terrier grinned and wriggled into her good arm. Scratching his ears, Faye looked around her room. The door was ajar.

"Good morning, Grandma."

Lucy March poked her head around the door. "Oh, you're awake. Morning, sleepyhead. How's the shoulder?"

Faye tested the strapping around her upper body. "The same as yesterday. Sore."

"You're going to feel sore for quite a few days. Nature's way of telling you to take it easy. That was quite a fall you took."

Before she could stop it, the entire scene replayed in Faye's head yet again: Exeter's grey ears snapping to attention as the plastic bag blew across the arena, the two jolting strides as he shied sideways. Still she urged him on to the obstacle before them, a triple combination. She remembered bracing her left arm, clamping her legs onto his sides. Exeter bunny-hopped the first jump, the vertical, landing short on the other side. Now their striding was off for the second jump, the oxer. Chirping and kicking she pushed him forward, asking him to stretch out, take a longer stride to bring them closer to the base of the wide jump of double rails. Confused, the young horse crouched down and leaped into the air.

He nearly made it. His front legs cleared the back rail of the oxer before his hind end was caught up, legs tangled in the striped poles. He dropped to the ground like a wounded bird. Faye was tossed clear before he landed, his thousand-pound body slamming against the grass with a force that rolled him onto his side. She sprawled beside Exeter, watching in horror as his enormous shoulder tipped toward her. She scrabbled at the ground, trying to squirm away, but it was too late. Her left shoulder was pinned beneath the horse.

"Exeter!" she screamed, and a big eye rolled at the sound of her voice. The young horse caught himself, kicked out to stop the momentum of his fall and was still.

Except for the rise and fall of his rib cage.

"Easy now, boy. You're okay," Faye soothed. "Everything's okay." *Please, let him be all right.*

She felt Exeter trembling, heard the rush of air blowing in and out of his nostrils in an increasing tempo, and knew the horse was as frightened as she was.

And then there was a voice—Patti, Exeter's groom, soothing the youngster. Abruptly the pressure on Faye's shoulder lifted as Exeter heaved up onto his sternum. She moved to sit up and fell back, gasping with pain. Her left shoulder was on fire, burning and throbbing. Her stomach heaved, her head spun.

Faye wrenched her mind back to the present. She swung her legs over the side of the bed. "I'm hungry. Really, really hungry."

"Your appetite's back. That's a good sign. You're on the mend."

"I want to get dressed. I'm sick of wearing Riley's T-shirts. I want to wear my own clothes."

"Here, let me help you."

"I can do it by myself. It's been over a week." She tested her shoulder, wincing only a little at the pain. "It feels a lot better."

"Don't push it, Faye. You heard the doctor: no riding for another month, at least."

Faye nodded, staring at her bare toes.

"Laurence Devries phoned last night after you were asleep. He said to tell you not to worry: Patty's going to keep the horses exercised. He was going to give them some time off anyway, so they'd be well rested for California. He said to get lots of rest and heal up good."

Faye let out a long sigh.

"I know you're disappointed, but it's not the end

of the world. Just a setback. Everything's going to be okay."

"Do you really think so?" She felt her grandmother's hand on her good shoulder and was comforted.

"I *know* so. It will all turn out for the best in the end. It always does."

Faye closed her eyes and let Lucy's words settle in.

"I'll go rustle up some breakfast for you." Lucy scooped Stubby off the bed and set him on the floor. Carefully, she wrapped an arm around her granddaughter and rested her faded strawberry-roan head on Faye's bright chestnut curls. "It'll be good to have you home for a while."

When her grandmother had gone, Faye looked around for her clothes. Her room was unusually tidy, everything stored away in drawers or the closet. More of her older brother's shirts were neatly stacked on top of her dresser.

The dresser had five drawers. The top three held polo shirts, breeches and jeans—all she ever wore. Clumsily yanking open the bottom drawer, she dug through the contents to discover a pair of black yoga pants. They would do.

By the time she was done getting out of pyjama bottoms and the oversized T-shirt and into clothes, she was exhausted. She was in another of Riley's shirts because she couldn't manage to pull any of her own over her injured shoulder. Her bedroom looked familiar again, clothes overflowing half-closed drawers.

She was looking for her slippers when a gust of wind rattled the dormer window. Outside, the old fir tree waved its needled branches in protest against the October storm, and clouds raced across the sky. Tricky weather for riding. The wind would have a horse on tiptoe, primed for a spook.

She turned away from the window with a sigh of relief. She wasn't going to be riding today, not in this weather. She wasn't going to be riding for a long time.

She found her slippers, put them on and dragged a damp brush through her hair, then picked up her sling and went downstairs.

"Better get a move on, Faye. We're picking up Kirsty and her mom in half an hour." Lucy set a plate of French toast on the table.

"What for?"

"The Equi-Fair, of course." Lucy gave her a sharp glance. "Did you forget?"

The doctor had told her grandmother that forget-fulness could be a sign of a concussion. Faye shook her head. "No, I just forgot that today is Saturday. Good thing you reminded me or I might have started doing schoolwork." This fall she'd begun home-schooling to fit in with her show jumping competition schedule.

"School's important, Faye."

"I know, I know," she said quickly. How many times had she heard that lecture? "I got a B on my social studies report. That's pretty good."

"You have been getting good marks lately."

"The Equi-Fair doesn't start until ten. Why are we going so early?"

"Linda and I are helping with the second-hand tack sale. All the proceeds are going to Safe Haven Horse and Pony Rescue. We have to set everything up."

"But Kirsty's mother doesn't know anything about saddles and bridles."

"You'd be surprised how much she's learned. Now that she knows some more about horses, she's not so afraid of them. Believe it or not, she's even gotten up on old Blackbird a few times. Hasn't done much more than walk around, but it's a start."

"Kirsty didn't tell me that."

"Oh, shoot! I forgot I wasn't supposed to tell anyone. Keep it a secret, okay? Linda wants to surprise her daughter."

"Sure. I can't believe it: Linda riding! It's amazing."

"It is. You just never know what people are going to do next."

Faye swirled a piece of French toast in syrup, wondering if this was the moment to tell Lucy. Before she could say anything, her grandmother pushed back her chair and carried her dishes to the sink. "We'll wash up later." She frowned at the sling. "You're not supposed to be using that thing anymore. Just for a few days, that's what the doctor said. It's important to start using your arm again, a little bit at a time."

"But I hurt too much without it on," protested Faye.

"Well, that's no good. Come on, girl, I'll help you with the sling. Then it's time to hit the road."

"Come in, come in! We're almost ready!" said Linda Hagen.

Lucy led the way into the Hagen kitchen and set a squirming Stubby on the floor. He scampered over to an elderly black Labrador retriever lying by the woodstove and licked him on the nose. The old dog thumped his tail in welcome.

"Is this okay?" Linda Hagen wore jeans and a snap button shirt, a bandana around her neck. Her hair was longer than the last time Faye had seen her, falling in soft waves to below her chin.

"You look fine, just fine, Linda. You'll fit right in," Lucy assured her.

"Faye!" Kirsty Hagen bounded down the stairs two at a time and threw her arms around her friend. "Oh, I'm sorry," she said as Faye gasped and pulled away. "Are you okay?"

Faye nodded. "Just don't touch my arm or shoulder."

"I won't, I promise. Oh, it must hurt so much."

"It does."

"Poor you. And you can't ride for how long?"

"A month, at least. Maybe more."

"That's terrible. And just when everything was going so good for you."

Faye shrugged. "Yeah, well, that's the way it goes." The truth was she'd forgotten all about her winning streak. The accident had put it clear out of her mind.

"So you're going to be home for at least a month. But you'll still be able to go down to California, won't you?" Kirsty asked as they climbed into her mother's little car.

"I...I don't know." She tried to keep the impatience out of her voice. "It's too soon to know anything for sure. I just have to wait and see."

"Right. Everything depends on how quickly your shoulder heals. Well, I'm sorry you're hurt but I'm glad you're home. I've missed you."

"Me too." It was true. Kirsty was the best friend Faye had ever had. When she'd started school in their small town, awkward and shy, the other kids had decided she was odd and had little to do with her. Year after year, grade after grade, she'd been a loner, counting the minutes until the final bell so she could go home to the farm and her beloved ponies. Then horse-crazy Kirsty had moved to Armstrong. Soon after, she got a pony, Lancelot. She kept him at the Marches' Hillcroft Farm and spent as much time there as she could. She admired Faye's riding skills and bragged of her success in the show jumping ring so much at school that the other kids began to see her in a new light. Now that Faye was away competing on Laurence Devries' horses, Kirsty had stepped in to fill her boots on the farm, helping Lucy with chores and even beginning to ride some of the ponies.

"We could go shopping one day, now that you're home," Kirsty said. "We could buy you some new clothes. You must get tired of wearing polo shirts and jeans all the time."

Faye tipped her head at her shoulder.

"Oh, right! I keep forgetting that you're injured."

I don't, thought Faye. *I never forget.*

"We can do something else, maybe go to a movie."

"That's a good idea," agreed Faye. "Let's do something else."

2

The parking lot at the fairgrounds in the centre of town was already filling up when Linda pulled in.

"The Equi-Fair doesn't open for another hour and a half," she said, locking the car doors. "All these vehicles must belong to exhibitors."

"It's become a big event," said Lucy. "Seminars, demonstrations, a trade show—anything and everything to do with horses. A lot of folks drive hours to get here. We're lucky that it's happening right in our backyard."

"I can't wait," said Kirsty. "I want to see everything! Midge Halliday is teaching about barrel racing. Faye, did you know she was a champion barrel racer a long time ago?"

Faye chewed her lip, trying to remember if she did or didn't.

Kirsty didn't wait for an answer. "There's going to be driving and reining and cutting exhibitions. Oh, and some lady is going to ride dressage in a sidesaddle. I've never seen anyone ride sidesaddle before. I want to see that one for sure."

"But first we have to set up for the tack sale," her

mother reminded her. "Lucy, do you know where we're supposed to go?"

"I sure do. We're under the main grandstand. Come on, ladies, follow me."

"So what's this contraption?" asked Linda, holding up a set of long leather straps. Two of the straps had rings on the ends.

"That's a running martingale," said Faye. "Put it right there, with the other ones."

Linda neatly arranged the martingale on the table next to the sign Kirsty had made. "I had no idea there was so much stuff you could put on a horse. All right, then, Faye, what are these things?"

"Bell boots."

"Really?" Linda gave the black rubber boots a shake. "But they don't make any noise. Are they broken?"

It took Faye a moment to catch on. "No, no, not that kind of bell!" She giggled. "They're called bell boots because they're shaped like bells. Sort of. Bells with the top ends chopped off. They fit like this." She pushed her hand through the top opening. "Pretend my hand is a hoof. See, the bell boot protects the bulbs of the horse's heel and the coronet band."

"I see," said Linda. "It's good to see you laugh, Faye."

"Hey, Faye, look what I've got." Kirsty dragged a cardboard box out from under a table. "A whole box of horse books. Some of them are really old. Look at the photographs in this one."

Faye knelt down beside her on the cement floor. Kirsty pointed to a black-and-white photograph of a man riding a horse over an enormous wall. She read the caption out loud: "'*Mr. Henry Zelinski on Valiant at the Royal Winter Fair in 1950 winning the Puissance at seven feet, two inches.*' Have you ever jumped that high, Faye?"

"Never. That's really, really high. It would take a special horse and rider to get over a jump that big."

"One day you will," Kirsty stated confidently. "I just know it."

Swallowing hard, Faye dug out another book. "We'd better get these priced and on the table. The doors are going to open any minute now."

"Wait a moment. These books could be really valuable because they're so old. Let me get my mom."

Linda looked quickly through the box. "Let's put these aside," she said. "I think it would be a good idea to have them valued by a book dealer."

"Opening time!" called Lucy. "Get ready, everyone, because here they come!"

A crowd spilled into the building. In minutes, the sale tables were surrounded. Lucy and Linda took money and made change while Kirsty and Faye looked after the tack.

A troupe of little girls clustered in front of the saddle pads. "Do you girls need help with anything?" asked Faye.

The girls dissolved into giggles.

"What's so funny?" called Kirsty from the other end of the booth.

"I don't know," Faye replied. "Girls?"

"You're Faye March, aren't you?" asked one of them. She held out an Equi-Fair program. "Will you sign this for me?"

"Oh! Sure. Uh, do you have a pen?"

More giggles. Kirsty found a pen and handed it to Faye. She wrote her name with a flourish on the program and passed it back. Suddenly another four or five programs were thrust under her nose.

"Did you break your arm?" someone asked.

Faye shook her head. "I sprained a joint in my shoulder."

"Does it hurt?"

Faye nodded. "A lot."

"But you'll get better."

"I will." She was still nodding.

"And then you'll go back to jumping."

Faye's bobbing head slowed. She signed the last program. "Here you are."

"Thank you, Faye," the girls chorused. Still laughing, they scurried away, glancing back at her over their shoulders.

"You're famous," said Kirsty, coming up beside Faye.

Faye closed her eyes and sighed. "Don't say that."

"What's wrong?"

She had to talk to someone. Who better than her best friend? She paused, searching for the right words.

"Hi there, everyone!" A stocky man in his sixties in a cowboy hat and boots came up to the booth.

Kirsty's attention was instantly diverted. "Oh, hi, Stuart! How's everything at the ranch?"

"Good, good. Had another phone call from someone who's thinking about adopting a pony for driving. He's coming out next week."

"Well, if it all works out, that will be the third pony adopted from Safe Haven in as many months," said Linda. "Good work, Stuart."

"Good work all of us. Now, I'm here to give a hand. What can I do?"

"Take over from Faye," instructed Linda. "You take a break, Faye, and give that shoulder some rest. Oh, and watch out for that box of books. We'd better push it farther under the table before one of us trips over it."

"I'll do it," Faye offered. The box was too heavy to move with her foot so she crouched down and shoved at it with her good arm. The box wobbled and tipped over. Books spilled onto the floor. Grumbling, Faye pushed the books under the table before anyone could step on them. She righted the box and settled it into place. It was too far to reach to replace the books in the box. She sighed and crawled under the table on her good hand and knees.

"Let me help you." Stuart knelt down and began picking up books and setting them back in the box.

One book, smaller than the others, lay right beside Faye's knee. She fumbled at it with one hand, and three photographs fluttered out, picture side down. Carefully, she lifted up the photos, pausing to read the handwriting on the back of the top one:

Mary Inglis on Colleen.

"There, all done. Let me help you up, Faye." Stuart caught her good elbow and pulled her to her feet.

"Excuse me! Hello? Could someone help me with these girths?" a woman called.

"Coming through!" Kirsty squeezed past, bumping Faye's good arm. "Whoops, sorry. Are you okay?"

"I'm fine," said Faye, hastily tucking the photos back into the book before they were knocked out of her hand.

There wasn't enough room for all of them in the booth. Faye squeezed through the gap between the tables. She knew it was silly, but she couldn't help feeling like she'd been kicked out.

"Faye! Here you go." Lucy reached across the table to press a bill into her hand. "Get yourself some lunch."

"I could bring lunch for all of you," Faye offered.

"How would you carry it?" said Lucy. "Don't worry about us, we'll manage."

"I'll come back soon."

"Take your time," said Linda. "There's no sense in overdoing it, just when you're getting better."

"That's right, Faye, we've got lots of help," Kirsty said.

"I'm here for most of the day," said Stuart. "Midge's barrel-racing seminar is one of the last events."

"Could you come back then, so I can go to the barrel racing?" asked Kirsty.

"Sure," said Faye. "Whatever." She turned away, blinking hard.

A few steps away from the Safe Haven Tack Sale booth and she was packed into a crowd of slow-moving bodies wandering through the building with frequent pauses to gaze at the displays. As soon as she saw an exit, she broke away. It wasn't until she was outside that she realized she was still carrying the book.

Some time later, she found herself climbing to the top tier of seating in the Agriplex, carrying a chicken wrap and a homemade lemonade in a box the concession worker had kindly found for her. The little book was tucked into her sling. She blew the dust off the hard bench and sat down with a sigh of relief. Ever since she'd left the tack booth she had been answering questions, many of them from people she was certain she didn't know. *What does it feel like to jump so high?* Like flying over the moon. *Do you get homesick?* Sometimes. *You're so brave to jump those big fences.* Just smile and nod and say nothing.

Because how could she tell the truth?

Faye closed her eyes and bowed her head in shame. Instantly she realized her mistake. The image of Exeter's huge body rolling toward her flashed through her brain yet again. Her stomach twisted, squeezing a sour taste up into the back of her throat. Her heart was suddenly racing, her teeth chattering. A flush of heat left sweat prickling at the back of her neck.

Just when she thought it would burst out of her chest, her heart slowed. She forced her eyes open and gulped deep breaths of air. Snatching up her drink, she washed away the bitter taste of bile. She glanced around but there were no curious looks coming her way. Nobody had noticed. She was okay.

Until the next time.

I won't think about it, Faye told herself. *I won't let myself remember and then it won't happen.* But it seemed the more she tried to turn off that part of her mind, the more the images flashed through her brain.

Think of something else! Anything! Down below, on the arena floor, workers were setting up an obstacle course. Handlers with miniature horses were gathering at the entrance. Faye shifted restlessly, willing the workers to hurry so the competition would start and distract her from the video clip that wouldn't stop playing in her memory. The little book jostled out of her sling and fell onto her knees. The front cover flipped open.

My Diary. Mary Louise Inglis, fourteen years old.

Even as her eyes were reading the handwriting on the flyleaf, Faye's fingers were turning the page.

3

June 4, 1955

Today I ran into the new ranch manager.

I really did. I'd turned Colleen for home and let her go so I wouldn't be late for supper again. We were halfway across the calving pasture when a man jumped the fence and came running across the field. I took hold of the reins, trying to figure out what he was doing, but Colleen wasn't stopping. Not for one moment did I think he'd get in the way of a galloping horse, but that's exactly what he did. He stopped right in front of us, waving his arms and hollering "whoa, whoa." Colleen ducked, trying to get around him, but the crazy man followed and grabbed one of her reins.

Mary could have told him that was a stupid thing to do. Colleen hated having her mouth pulled on, so when she felt that tug on the rein, she tossed her head high in the air. At the same time her chest hit the man's shoulder and knocked him to the ground, right into a nice, fresh cow patty.

Mary turned Colleen in circles to get a good look at the crazy man so she could tell her father all about him. She made sure to stay well away because he was already up on his feet. There was a long green smear across his face. He wasn't swearing like she'd expected, and he stood real straight with his chin up. He wasn't anyone she knew from the ranch.

"Mister, I don't know who you are or what kind of trouble you're out to cause, but you'd better get those fancy boots of yours moving fast because my dad's the head wrangler on this ranch and I'm going straight home to tell him what you just did, and if he finds you still hanging around...well, you'll be sorry. Believe me, you will."

Then she headed in the opposite direction, to the far corner of the pasture by the old-timers' graveyard. That meant jumping over the wooden gate onto the road. Colleen cleared it like a deer, but Mary slid up onto her neck when she came down and had to grab mane to hang on. When the horse felt her slipping she stopped, as she always did, and waited for Mary to regain her seat.

Mary looked back, and the man was still standing

there in the pasture, looking their way. But when Dad got out there a little while later, the man was gone.

"Tell me what he looked like," Dad said as he walked back across the field, the tired grass crunching under his boots. Colleen lazed alongside him on a long rein, Mary's legs dangling down her sides. At this time of the year, early June, the cows and their white-faced babies had been turned out onto the mountain ranges surrounding the ranch. Only a few late-calving heifers remained, pastured close to the ranch yard while they waited for their first babies to be born.

"He was a bit taller than you, Dad, and his hair was cut real short. Well, I think it was, because he was wearing a hat. Not a straw hat like yours but some sort of flat cap." She paused, trying hard to remember why the stranger had looked so different from the cowboys and ranch hands she saw every day. "He had a tie."

"A tie? Are you sure?"

She nodded. Dad lifted his own hat clear of his head and settled it right back down again, the way he always did when he was thinking hard.

"I'll tell the other men to look out for him. C'mon, I've got to turn out the horses, and then we'll get ourselves some supper." Dad led the way into the ranch yard, the direction Mary had been taking before the stranger appeared.

She stood Colleen in the shade of a lean-to while Dad swung open the gate to the big corral so the ranch horses could head out into the home pasture and spend the night grazing.

"Hello there!" a man's voice called out, and the stranger emerged from the shadows of the big barn.

"Dad! It's him! It's the crazy man," Mary shouted, pointing to the stranger.

The man spun around and began marching toward her. The green smear on his face had been wiped off. "Excuse me, young lady, I certainly do not appreci-ate—" The man broke off as Dad scrambled over the corral fence and came running at him.

"Stop right there!" Dad grabbed the knot of the man's tie and shook it. "You stay away from my girl, you hear me?"

"Let go of me this instant!"

"Henry! What's going on?" A young woman hurried from the barn, followed by Joe Pettit. The cow boss took in the situation at a glance. He grabbed Dad's arms from behind, breaking his grip on the stranger's tie.

"Joe, you let me go." Dad struggled but the cow boss had his arms securely pinned. "I'm telling you—"

"No, Donny, I'm telling *you*: this is Mr. Henry Zelinski. Mr. Dalton sent him. Meet the new ranch manager."

Dad froze. "Let go," he repeated quietly, and Joe did so. Dad looked all around: up at the cloudless sky, over at the blue-shadowed mountains, up and down and along the old barn, as if he was measuring it for repainting. Finally he bowed his head, studying the scuffed toes of his boots. Up went the straw hat, then back down again.

Mary found she was trembling, sick with horror at the situation. Colleen chose that moment to sidle restlessly out of the dark cover of the lean-to's shade. The new manager looked over at her with a frown. He turned back to Dad.

"And you are?"

Dad lifted his head. "Donald Inglis, sir."

"He's our head wrangler, Mr. Zelinski, and the best hand with horses you'll find in this country. Donny can gentle any horse," said Joe. "And he does it real quiet. None of that bucking bronco stuff, not at all. When Donny's finished with him, that horse wants to go to work, he gets him to like it so much."

Henry Zelinski nodded. Abruptly, he held out his hand. "Pleased to meet you, Mr. Inglis. I'm sure we'll have lots to discuss. Horses are a particular interest of mine."

Dad gave the new manager a long, hard look before shaking his hand. "Everyone calls me Donny. That's what I've gotten used to answering to."

The woman stepped up to the manager's side. "Henry? Is everything all right?"

"It is now, dear. A misunderstanding but we've cleared it up. Donny, this is my wife, Dorothy."

"Pleased to meet you, Mrs. Zee...Mrs. Zuh...ah, I'm sorry. I'm not real good with names."

"It's a real tongue twister," said Dorothy Zelinski. "Please, just call me Mrs. Zee."

"Will do. Mr. Zee, about that misunderstanding? I owe you an explanation," Dad began, but Dorothy was tugging at her husband's hand.

"Henry, look at this mare. I know, I know, her condition's a bit rough, but have you ever seen such a beautiful neck and well-set hocks." She tipped her head back and smiled up at Mary. "That's a fine-looking palomino you're on. Part Thoroughbred, is she?"

Mary shrugged and gave the answer she'd been taught. "I don't know. She came from the wild horses out on the range. Dad got her for me when I was little. He broke her, but I've done all her training since then."

"Oh, so you must be...?"

"I'm Mary. Mary Inglis. I'm his daughter." She jerked her chin toward her father.

"This is the girl on the runaway," said Henry Zelinski.

"Colleen doesn't run away," Mary retorted. "She likes to go fast so sometimes I let her."

"And how often is sometimes?"

Mary twirled Colleen's white mane in her fingers. "Once a day. Maybe twice."

"And do you never use a saddle?" asked Dorothy Zelinski.

"Sometimes. Well, not often. I've only got a stock saddle. It's not very good to jump in. One day I'm going to get a real jumping saddle, one of those English ones."

Dad snorted in disgust. "Pancake saddles!"

"You mean you jump your mare bareback?" asked Dorothy, widening her dark blue eyes. "Can you believe that, Henry?"

"Yes, I can. I've seen it happen with my own eyes. A solid board fence, close to five feet high. The mare cleared it as if she had wings."

"And the child stayed on?"

"She most certainly did." Henry Zelinski shook his head. "Mary, I owe you an apology."

"You do? For what?"

"Let me explain. My wife and I just arrived at the ranch this afternoon, a half day ahead of schedule."

"He drives his car like you ride your mare," Dorothy said to Mary, behind her hand.

"I heard that, my dear."

"It's nothing but the truth. Henry, you do have a love for speed." Dorothy linked her arm through her husband's and grinned up at him. The corners of the manager's mouth stretched to return the smile.

"As I was saying, I was walking around, getting to know the lay of the land, when I heard the hoof-beats of a galloping horse. I ran to investigate and saw a child on a palomino horse going at full speed across the wide open field toward the ranch yard. I assumed what I was seeing was an out-of-control horse bolting for home. So, naturally, I took action."

Mary frowned, recalling the man running directly into the path of her galloping mare, waving his arms and grabbing for the reins. "So you were trying to stop Colleen from running away with me."

Henry nodded. "I was."

"You could have been run over, you know."

"I thought you were in danger. I was trying to help."

Mary stared at him, trying to understand how she could be at any kind of risk atop her beloved mare.

"Thank you, sir," said Dad. "That was a brave thing you did. Mary, say thank you."

"But, Dad, Colleen wasn't running away. She wouldn't do that, not to me. And he shouldn't go around saying she did."

Dad lifted his hat and ran his hand through his dark hair. He set his hat back in place. "Sorry, Mr. Zee, for my girl's bad behaviour. She's a stubborn one."

"But it's true! She wasn't doing anything wrong," protested Mary. She narrowed her eyes right back at her father's glare. "Oh, all right." She heaved a sigh. "Sorry."

Silently, she added…*that you got it wrong about Colleen taking off with me and caused all this fuss.*

Henry Zelinski looked up at Mary, sitting on her mare with her arms crossed and brows knotted in a fierce frown. "I accept your apology, young lady. Now then, Donny, fill me in regarding the ranch horses."

"You bet, Mr. Zee."

"Dad, I'm going home." Without waiting for an answer, Mary spun Colleen around and trotted away.

4

How had things turned out for Mary Inglis and her horse? Faye had to know. She lifted the top corner of the page with her finger to turn it over and paused. This was someone's—Mary Inglis's—diary. It was meant to be private.

She should respect that privacy.

Leaving the page unturned, she put the little book beside her on the bench and reached for her lunch. Once again, the three photographs slid out from between the pages of the book. Faye found herself looking at the black-and-white photo of a girl, hatless, with her hair tugged back into dark braids that hung over her shoulders. Her dark eyes were on the palomino mare beneath her, her hands wrapped in the thick, white mane. The mare's head was lifted high, gazing off into the distance with that fathomless expression horsemen call "the look of eagles." She wore neither bridle nor saddle, and the girl's thin legs dangled down her sides. Faye turned the photograph over.

Mary Inglis on Colleen.

Imagine jumping fences and gates—bareback! Mary Inglis would have been a fearless rider, Faye decided. She'd ridden a lot without a saddle herself, all over Hillcroft Farm, but it had never occurred to her to try and jump the ponies over the pasture gates. Mary must have had incredible balance to stay aboard while her horse soared over the obstacles. She would have trusted her mare, Colleen, implicitly. There had to have been an unusually strong bond between horse and rider; from the first page of Mary's diary that was obvious.

Faye swallowed hard. She loved all the ponies on their farm, but there was one she'd felt a special kinship with, her wonderful Hillcroft Red Robin. Only he wasn't hers anymore. Valuable as a successful jumper, he'd been sold to save the farm. Faye missed him every day.

In the next photo, a man and a woman sat astride a pair of horses, bays or dark chestnuts, Faye couldn't tell because once again the photo was in black and white. The woman was riding in a western saddle. She was laughing into the camera, lifting her straw hat in the air to reveal blonde hair tucked up in a French roll. Her laughter contrasted sharply with the stern face of the man beside her. He sat his mount with a disciplined elegance. Faye could tell by the relaxed stance of his horse that his hands were gentle on the reins. She checked the back of the photo.

Dorothy Zelinski on Vega, Mr. Henry Zelinski on Valiant. Heading out on the trails, White Valley Ranch, 1955.

Faye slid the third photograph out from under the other two. It took her several moments to realize the pale-coloured mare soaring over the enormous brick wall, her rider's arms stretched to give her all the rein she needed, was Colleen. Her mane was neatly braided and her golden coat gleamed under the artificial lights of the indoor riding arena. The rider was outfitted in the regulation show jumping uniform of the day— black velvet-covered helmet, long dark riding coat, white breeches and tall black leather to-the-knee boots. A single dark braid flew out the back of her helmet. Slowly, Faye flipped the photo to the other side.

Colleen, Pacific National Exhibition, 1955. Rider Mary Inglis.

How did a ranch horse and her young rider go from jumping bareback around the ranch to competing in the PNE just a few months later? The desire to find out was too strong to resist. Faye reached for the little book and, once again, began to read.

June 16, 1955

Saturday, so no school. Yippee! Got out early before Dad and Tom were even up. Colleen and I went up the mountain to our favourite place. You can see out over the whole valley from up there. When the sun had everything warmed up good, Colleen lay down for a nap. She looked so pretty, all golden and gleaming with green grass and purple wildflowers all around her. I sat down with her and she curled her neck right around me. It was like getting a giant hug.

One day I'm going to get a foal from Colleen. She'll be a good mom. She'll take good care of her baby. She won't go away and leave it behind.

We looked around for the wild herd but couldn't find them. They must be far back in the mountains looking for fresh grass. It's better if they stay up high and keep away from the ranch hayfields.

We came home about noon. My stomach wouldn't quit growling. Too bad I couldn't eat grass, like Colleen.

When we rode into the yard, Mrs. Zee was there, sitting on an apple box beside the back door.

"Hello there!" she called out.

"Hi," Mary muttered. She slid off Colleen and stared at the toes of her boots. What the heck was Dorothy Zelinski doing here?

"I saw your father was working this morning, so I thought I'd come and keep you company."

Mary lifted her gaze to stare at the young woman. They were far apart in age, at least a dozen, maybe fifteen years. What were they going to have in common?

"If that's okay with you," Dorothy added.

Mary shrugged. "Guess so."

She unbuckled the halter and slipped it off Colleen's head. The palomino followed her to the corner of the veranda where she stowed her horse gear. Mary selected a soft brush and set to work removing the dried sweat from her mare's wheat-straw-coloured hair. Colleen grunted with pleasure, her dark eyes half closed. She shifted a haunch into the pressure of the brush, encouraging Mary to rub harder into the thick muscles.

"That feels good, eh." Forgetting Dorothy Zelinski's presence, she hummed in time with the rhythm of the brush strokes.

When she was done brushing, she combed the pale silky mane and ran her fingers through the long tail, separating the tangles, careful not to yank and break any hairs. She ran a soft cloth over the mare's entire body, finishing off by gently wiping the blaze that ran down the centre of the finely chiselled head. "That's it, my queen."

Colleen bowed her head and wandered away to eat the grass standing tall in the shelter of the house.

Mary hosed off all her brushes and the rub rag and laid them out in a sunny spot on the veranda floor to dry. Then she squared her shoulders and turned back to Dorothy Zelinski. "I'm done."

"Have you had lunch? Would you like me to make you something to eat?"

At the mention of food, Mary's stomach rumbled, loud and clear. "No, thank you, I can fix my own lunch." She climbed the three steps onto the veranda. The woman made no move to leave.

"May I come in?" she asked.

Then Mary understood. She knew the purpose of this visit. It was an inspection. They'd had them many times before, the wives on the ranch dropping in with a plate of cookies or a jar of jam—"I'll just put this on the table"—so they could have a quick look around at the condition of things inside the house.

She knew if she said no, Mrs. Zelinski would go away even more suspicious, but she hadn't expected a visitor and truly the house was a mess. Yesterday's dishes were piled in the sink, today's on the counter; dirt crunched underfoot on the linoleum floor; and the windows were dull with a film of smoke from the woodstove that had been burning all winter.

Tugging open the screen door, she waved Dorothy Zelinski inside without looking back.

"My, this is cozy," Dorothy said, not even trying to hide her curiosity as she looked around.

Mary pulled a chair away from the kitchen table and sat down to pull off her boots. "Sorry for the mess," she said, without meaning it. "I'm cleaning up this afternoon."

"It must be hard to keep up with everything. This is a very busy household, isn't it? Let's see if I remember correctly: your father is the head wrangler; your brother, Tom, is a cowboy; and you're still in school. Have I got it right?"

Mary nodded. What was all this leading up to? She set her boots neatly on the newspaper by the door and went to the sink to wash her hands. "We don't have a mother. She passed away when I was three."

Better to get it out in the open, she'd found. People would spend all day dancing around the subject, dropping hints here and there, when really it was all they wanted to talk about.

"I'd heard that," Dorothy Zelinski admitted. "I'm

sorry, that must have been difficult for your family. Your father did a good job, raising two fine children."

Mary liked how she called them a family, even though there wasn't a mother involved. "He's a good dad." She opened the refrigerator. "Want a sandwich?"

"That would be lovely. What can I do to help?"

"I can manage. Just have a seat."

"All right, then, I will."

There was a long silence. Spreading mustard on the roof of a salami sandwich, Mary peeked over her shoulder. The woman was gazing out the window beside the table, lost in thought. Mary filled the kettle and put it on the stove.

"Tell me about Colleen," said Dorothy. "How old is she?"

"Seven. Or around about that. I don't know exactly because she's off the range." Mary clamped her lips together after telling the lie. She knew exactly how old her horse was. And she should; Colleen had been with her since she was just a few months old.

"The range? So she was born wild. That surprises me. She's got such quality about her, I was sure she had some Thoroughbred blood in her."

Mary kept her eyes fixed on the kettle.

"And how did you get her?"

"Like I said before, Dad got her for me. When I was little. If you want to know any more, you'll have to ask him." She snatched up the boiling kettle, and water sloshed out of the spout.

"Mary, be careful!" Dorothy rose, took the kettle from her and poured the water into the teapot. Setting the kettle down, she placed her hand on Mary's arm. "Did I say something to upset you?"

Mary shook her head and shrugged. She breathed in Dorothy's faint floral scent. She caught the thread of a faint memory. Carefully, she tugged at the thread, pulling the memory closer: she was little, held in a woman's arm, her head resting on a narrow shoulder, a hand gently stroking her hair. The scent of lily of the valley filling her nostrils.

Abruptly the thread broke. She'd pulled too hard again.

"Are you all right?" Dorothy asked.

Mary blinked hard. "I'm fine. Just hungry."

"Then you should eat. Come, sit down."

Dorothy Zelinski picked up the plate of sandwiches. Her fingernails were buffed and shiny with clear nail polish.

Mary set the pot of tea and a pair of mugs on the table. The pot was too full, and tea dribbled out the spout onto the Formica tabletop. She brought over a jug of milk and the sugar bowl and dropped down into the chair opposite her guest.

"Shall I pour?" asked Dorothy.

"Yes, please." Mary took a sandwich and bit into it.

"Milk?"

Mouth full, Mary nodded.

"Tell me when." Dorothy poured milk into one of

the mugs until Mary nodded. She finished chewing and swallowed.

"Thank you."

"You're very welcome."

There was another long gap without words. It was so quiet Mary could hear herself chewing. Her face flushed. Her hand, reaching for another sandwich, paused.

"If you're hungry you should eat," said Dorothy Zelinski. "You work hard."

Colleen whinnied at the window beside the table. Pushing her chair back, Mary got up and shoved the window open. The mare extended her head into the room and gently inspected all the items on the table.

"Welcome! Come to join the tea party, have you?" Dorothy chuckled.

The mare knocked over the sugar bowl.

"Hey, none of that." Mary scooped up the sugar and removed the bowl. "I'll get your carrot."

"This is no ordinary horse. You know that, don't you?"

"Yes, Mrs. Zee, I sure do."

"Please, call me Dorothy. And you're a very pretty girl when you smile."

Mary's cheeks warmed. She broke a carrot into pieces and set them on the table close to the window. One by one, Colleen lipped up each chunk and crunched it between her strong teeth. She sighed with pleasure.

"You know, Mary, when I said that Colleen is

extraordinary I wasn't just talking about her social skills. I also meant her jumping ability. Who taught her to jump?"

"Me. I did."

"Oh my goodness! And who taught you to jump?"

"No one. I just started doing it. First on my pony, Mike, and then on Colleen. We started over logs and then the feed bunks. One day we came across a section of fence and the top rail had fallen down. Colleen took that real easy so we came back over the whole fence. I was a bit nervous because it looked so high so I closed my eyes, but Colleen, she just flew. And now..." Mary grinned. "Well, now that fence doesn't look like anything. Now we just jump over everything we come across. Once—and you might not believe this but it's true—we jumped over this little sports car belonging to the old boss's son. Nobody saw and I would've been in big trouble if they had, but we really did."

"Oh, I believe you."

"But you haven't seen Colleen jump. I could be doing a bunch of bragging for all you know."

"My husband has seen her. Henry hasn't been so impressed by a horse for a long time. And he knows a good jumper when he sees one. He's ridden a lot of very good horses, you see, and won jumping classes at all the big shows in Canada and the United States. He's even competed in England and Europe. Are you sure you've never heard of Henry Zelinski?"

Mary shook her head. She hadn't known there were

big shows with jumping classes in North America. And she'd never imagined travelling all the way overseas to ride in horse shows.

"You're very isolated here on the ranch so I suppose I shouldn't be surprised. Back east everyone knows who he is. That's how we came here—the ranch owners, Mr. and Mrs. Dalton, heard from a friend that Henry was retiring from competition and offered him the position of manager. It's much too soon for him to retire, but he'd suffered so many disappointments trying to find another Valiant—he's been Henry's very best horse—that something went out of him. Until now, until he saw Colleen. He's shown more enthusiasm for that lovely mare than he has for anything or anyone for a long time. Maybe even me."

Mary shook her head, recalling Henry Zelinski's look of adoration for his wife.

"Have you ever competed with Colleen in a horse show?"

"No, ma'am."

"Oh, you should. She's a natural. With the right training she could be a winner."

"That's what I want to do," Mary confided. "I want to jump Colleen in a horse show. I just don't know how to go about it."

"That's exactly what I wanted to talk to you about." Dorothy leaned across the table. "Mary, you know the old saying about how a green rider and a green horse don't mix?"

"Yes," she replied warily.

"Henry could teach Colleen so much. She could benefit from his years of experience. He could take her places, to the very best horse shows in Canada and the United States. Colleen could be at the Pacific National Exhibition, the Royal Winter Fair, Madison Square Garden. Who knows, maybe she's good enough to go to Europe. Wouldn't that be something?" Dorothy bounced in her seat.

Mary's head was whirling. "What about school?"

"Hmm?"

"I've got to go to school. How could I do that if I'm at all these horse shows?"

"Oh, no, you wouldn't be riding. Henry would."

Mary frowned, still confused.

"Mary, what I mean is we would buy Colleen from you. At a very fair price, of course. Enough money to pay for all your university education when you're done high school."

"But I wouldn't have Colleen."

"You could buy another horse. Horses."

"I don't want any other horse."

"Colleen has so much talent. It's just going to go to waste if she doesn't get the right training. Henry can give her that training, Mary, he—"

"No!" Mary's chair fell over as she stood up abruptly. "She's not for sale!"

"Mary, please listen. Come back!"

She was out the door, rushing around the house to

her beloved mare. Colleen startled a little, her head lifting high, but she held still as Mary grabbed a hank of mane and swung herself aboard. Then they were off, hopping over the rickety picket fence into the pasture beyond, over the split rails and up, up into the rolling blue mountains slumbering alongside the ranch, where the evergreens would lower their needled branches to hide them away.

5

"There you are," said Dad when Mary finally came home. "Tom and I were talking about putting together a search party to come look for you." He was sitting at the kitchen table, his stockinged feet up on the chair opposite.

Mary glanced at the wall clock. It was past eight o'clock in the evening. The June light was still full strength.

Tom was at the sink, washing dishes. He picked up a plate and carefully wiped one side and then the other with the dishcloth. His hands were big and muscled like their father's but still smooth skinned. He was eighteen and had left school last year to work on the ranch. "You didn't leave a note. You're supposed to tell us where you're going."

He was right. "Sorry." Mary pulled off her boots. She picked up the dishtowel.

"Wash your hands first," said Tom. "No, not in the dishwater. In the bathroom, like a civilized human being." He gave one of her braids a tug with a soapy hand as she turned to go.

"Hey, cut that out! Dad!"

"Settle down, you two."

In the bathroom, Mary studied her reflection in the mirror as she soaped her hands. She practised a smile. Pretty? She wasn't sure. Her eyebrows were dark slashes over her eyes, and her cheekbones were sharp and high. Her nose was all right, but her chin was too square.

She rinsed her hands and dried them, trying to rub away the unsettling feeling that had come over her. Thinking about being pretty had made her recall all the other things Dorothy Zelinski had said.

She charged back into the kitchen and flung her arms around her father.

"Hey, hey, what's all this?" Dad stroked her head like she was a timid foal.

Mary shook her head against his shoulder. It would take too many words to explain why she was upset. Dad said nothing more for a long while, his hand gently resting on her head.

"Did you turn your mare out in the big pasture?" he asked. "She's put in a long day; she'll need the extra feed."

"I did." Mary straightened. The remains of her lunch had been pushed to one corner of the table to make way for Tom's and Dad's supper. She began picking up the mugs and plates.

"Looks like you had company today," Dad observed.

Pursing her lips, Mary nodded.

"Mrs. Zee?"

"You knew she was coming? Did you know what for?"

"Uh-huh. She asked me about the horse. I told her she'd have to talk to you."

"Why didn't you just tell her no?"

"Figured you're old enough now to say it for yourself." Dad squinted at her. "Is that why you're so wound up? You're mad about Mrs. Zee asking to buy your horse for her husband?"

"Yes! I am! She's my horse and she's not for sale."

"Well, that's all you had to tell her. Get used to it, Mary. A horse like your Colleen doesn't come along very often. Anyone who's been around horses at all knows how rare the good ones are. It probably won't be the last offer you get to buy her."

"And I'm going to say no to all of them!"

"Well, youngster, that's your choice. Just do one thing for me: be polite in your saying no. Just like I hope you were with Mrs. Zee today."

Mary spun away and marched to the sink with the dirty dishes.

"Mary?"

"I'll apologize tomorrow. Okay?"

"Okay. In the future try holding your tongue before you speak. Then you won't end up having to hand out so many apologies. At least, that's what I've found."

"I tried, Dad, I really tried, but she kept asking all these questions."

"What kind of questions?" asked Tom.

"About Colleen. How old she is, where she came from, that kind of thing."

"And what did you tell her?" asked their father.

"That she was around seven years old and off the range. Then I told her if she wanted to know any more to ask you."

"You said all the right things. Now put it aside and quit fretting."

"But, Dad, what if she finds out?"

"She won't. Nobody else has. Stop worrying about it so much, Mary. Everything's just fine. Now, you'd better go out and water the garden or those vegetables aren't going to grow. And what about the weeding? Did you do any today?"

"I was too busy."

"I'm going to try that line sometime," said Tom. "Sorry, boss, didn't get those cows moved because I was too busy."

"Mary, I know you don't like weeding, but the job's still got to be done. Understand?" said Dad.

She sighed and nodded. "I do."

June 17, 1955

I'm going to have to do this. I sure don't want to. Just thinking about it makes my stomach hurt. But I know Dad wants me to and I'm not going to let him down.

The prospect of apologizing to Dorothy Zelinski squirmed inside Mary like a garter snake. It got so bad that, late Sunday afternoon, she haltered her old pony, Mike, and looped the lead rope around his neck, tying the free end to his halter to act as a rein.

"You can have a rest," she told Colleen when the golden mare came running across the field to her. That was only part of the reason for leaving Colleen behind. The other was she didn't want to tempt the Zelinskis with the sight of the mare. She swung aboard Mike and rode down to the big house.

No one answered her knock at the front door. She headed for the back door, leading Mike alongside. Partway there, the pony's ears snapped to alert and his nostrils fluttered. Instinctively, Mary clapped a hand over his nose, cutting off the whinny that was about to burst out. The pony shook his head, annoyed, his attention still fixed on the far side of the house.

"You hush now," Mary hissed. She made her way to the corner of the house, pulling Mike with her, careful to tread on the grass lawn instead of the gravel path. She wasn't certain why she felt this need for secrecy, except that she liked to know the lay of the land before she went into any situation. She peered around the corner through the leafy branch of a lilac bush gone wild. The lead was tugged through her hand as the pony shoved his head down to crop the tender green grass. Food came first in Mike's life, any time, any place.

There were two horses dancing on the back lawn

of the big house. Side by side, they pranced in place, necks curved and tails arched high, their riders tall and slim on their backs. As Mary watched, the horses moved away from each other, lifting each leg higher and putting it down slowly until there was a half-beat pause between each stride. Mary knew the riders were directing their mounts with barely perceptible signals, but the horses seemed to be playing, revelling in their power and grace and agility.

One rider barked a command, and now the pair was cantering. Oh, but what cantering—this rocking-horse gait, barely stirring the riders in their saddles, while beneath them, shiny, sharp-edged hooves flashed in rhythmical unison over the ground.

"Extend!" At the command, the horses stretched forward, their bodies lengthening, their hooves kicking up divots of dirt as they charged down opposite sides of the lawn. In the corners they changed shape again, their heads and necks lifting high, backs compressing, strides contracting until they were barely moving over the grass. Together, both horses turned, skipped down the centre of the lawn beside each other and came to a halt, standing like statues right in the middle.

The sun shot through the trees, glinting off Dorothy Zelinski's golden hair as she turned to her husband, laughing. But Henry Zelinski wasn't looking at his wife. He was staring straight ahead at the lilac bush beside the corner of the house. He jutted his chin forward, squinting into the branches.

Mary ducked back.

"Hey! You there! Come out, right now!"

Pressed against the house, Mary could hear the soft thud of hooves on grass, coming closer.

"Henry, what is it?" called Dorothy.

"Somebody's there, watching us."

Mike stopped grazing. His head came up, nostrils fluttering.

"Mike, shhh. No, no, whoa!" she hissed. She made a grab for the pony's lead rope as he scooted past her, but he veered out of reach. Whinnying joyfully, he trotted around the corner of the house to greet the two horses.

"What on earth? Steady, Valiant, stand now. Why, you little devil! Watch out, Dot, he kicks."

"Henry, help me! Get him away! Whoa, Vega, whoa!"

Mary had to look. Dorothy's horse whirled in circles, terrified by the much smaller animal. With a pony's wicked sense of humour, Mike was trumpeting in triumph, striking with his front feet. He swapped ends and lashed out with his hind feet, sending the horse bolting to the far end of the lawn, where Dorothy managed to pull her up. Before the pony could cause more mischief, Mary burst out of hiding and snatched up his lead rope.

"You!" Henry Zelinski glared down at her. "Don't you let go of that wretched beast. It's all right, Dorothy, the pony's under control."

Dorothy urged the pop-eyed mare closer. "Mary? What are you doing here?"

"I came to apologize. For yesterday. I was rude. I'm sorry. And I'm sorry about what happened just now, too."

"Hmmph." Henry sniffed. "I can certainly understand why you need to apologize for letting that pony run loose. He's got a nasty temper, that one. Do you realize you could have caused a serious accident?"

"Of course I do! I've been around horses all my life. I just didn't think anyone would be riding on their back lawn."

"That does seem to be a common theme with you, doesn't it, young lady—you don't think."

"Mary! Thank you very much for coming over," said Dorothy.

"*You're* welcome. Goodbye. Come on, Mike." She dropped her voice to a whisper. "Bad pony! You shouldn't have done that. You're not the boss here, you know."

"One moment, please!" barked Henry.

Startled, Mary halted abruptly. Mike bumped into her shoulder.

"Please tell me what happened yesterday. I want to know."

"Oh, Henry, it was nothing. Just a...a bit of a mix-up, that's all," said Dorothy. "Nothing to worry about. Everything's sorted out now."

"*What* was nothing? *What* is nothing to worry

about? Dorothy, I am the manager of this ranch. I need to know what goes on here."

"Really, you're making such a to-do about this. All right, then; I went to see Mary yesterday to ask if she'd sell her mare to us."

"What?"

"I know, I know, I realize now that I shouldn't have, but I haven't seen you so enthused about a horse, about anything, in such a long time. I wanted you to be happy again. I didn't think there would be any harm in just asking."

"Oh, Dot." Henry sighed. "I know you meant well, but you should have talked this over with me first."

"I wanted it to be a surprise. A nice surprise. I'm so sorry, Mary, for upsetting you. I didn't think about your feelings and I should have. Please, will you forgive me?"

Mary stared at the toes of her boots. She wasn't accustomed to having an adult apologize to her. She answered with a shrug.

"Oh, thank you, Mary, I am so relieved. Please don't rush off. I've just promised Henry lemonade and cookies. You must stay and join us. We are done schooling, aren't we, dear?"

"Yes, that's enough for today."

"All right, then! First we'll put the horses away, and then cookies and lemonade on the lawn. We can talk horses."

After the horses—Valiant and Vega—had been turned out in their paddock, and Mike let loose to graze the lawn, they sprawled under a wild apple tree, crunching gingersnap cookies. Prodded by his wife, Henry told tales of his exploits with Valiant in the show jumping arena. He'd competed at faraway cities that Mary had only heard of, ridden in horse shows that she didn't know existed, and been taught with military discipline by riding masters with exotic names, who were trained in ancient traditions.

"My father was my first teacher and I couldn't have had a better instructor. He came from a well-off family. They had a very large farm in Poland, and he'd been in the cavalry before coming to Canada to take up farming. He was very strict, very demanding, but he taught me and my brothers and sisters well."

Henry's face was mobile as he talked, eyes gleaming, brows waggling. From time to time he even smiled. He spoke of courageous horses and skilful riders; of evening competitions before crowds of spectators, the women in gowns and jewels and furs, and the men in tuxedos; of long hours at practice, muscles cramping, calves and knees rubbed raw, until one magic day all the tension was simply gone and he became part of the horse. Two separate creatures in complete harmony. A whole new being greater than the sum of the parts.

"Then what?" breathed Mary. "What happened next?"

Henry sighed and tugged a handful of grass from the parched lawn. He and Valiant were at the pinnacle of their success. There was talk of them making the Olympic team for Helsinki, the first time civilians would be allowed to compete in the equestrian events that previously had only been open to military teams. Then Valiant came up lame with a serious tendon injury that needed time to heal. Months and months of time. "And that was that."

"What do you mean? Didn't Valiant get better?"

"He recovered, but not enough to return to his former level of competition. His leg will not stand up to the strain of jumping the big fences. Valiant's jumping career is over."

"That's awful. But why didn't you get another horse?"

"Oh, I've been looking, Mary. Even before Valiant was injured I had my eye out for another good jumper, but they're as rare as diamonds. For a while it looked as though Vega might fit the bill, but no, she's too easily discouraged if things go wrong. She hasn't got the heart for a top-level competitor. And now, if you ladies will pardon me, I think I'll close my eyes for a short rest."

Mary sat for some time in silence, her mind whirling with everything she'd heard. She sighed and turned to Dorothy. "I didn't know you could ride."

"Oh, yes. I grew up on a farm in Ontario. That's where I met Henry—he was teaching riding lessons at our local riding club. But I don't compete. I just don't have that kind of nerve. I fall apart in the show ring."

It was hard to imagine the self-assured Dorothy Zelinski falling apart over anything. "Your horse is beautiful. That trick you were doing on her, you know, when she was prancing on the spot—how do you get her to do that?"

Roused from his nap, Henry sat up to glare at her. "That was no trick! The movement is called piaffe, and it's the result of systematic training and development of the horse's physique based on the natural movements of the horse."

"I didn't know."

"Of course you didn't," said Dorothy. "How could you? Henry, stop looking so ferocious! You're frightening us. It's part of dressage, Mary. It's a way of training the horse that goes back to the ancient Greeks. When it's done properly, the horse becomes a willing partner with the rider. Isn't that right, Henry?"

"In simple terms, I suppose it is. In very simple terms."

"Is it hard to do?" asked Mary.

"Hard to do?" He repeated her words slowly. "I don't think you quite understand. What you saw today is the result of years of practice and study."

"Any horse can benefit from being taught the basics of dressage," said Dorothy.

"Even Colleen?" asked Mary.

"Especially that mare of yours," said Henry.

"Consistent training would help her become more supple, more balanced and certainly more obedient."

Mary shook her head. "I don't want her spirit broken."

"Young lady, have you listened? I am talking about working with the horse's willing cooperation, not beating her into behaving," he huffed. "Your horse has all the jumping ability in the world, but she is barely under control. With the right training she'd work with you instead of fighting you like a wild mustang."

"She *does* work with me!" Mary scrambled to her feet.

"Mary, please don't run off, not like this," pleaded Dorothy. "Henry didn't mean to upset you."

"I've got to go. My dad told me not to be too long." She tugged Mike's head away from his grazing. "Thank you for the cookies. The lemonade, too. It was very good."

There, she'd remembered her manners. She vaulted onto Mike and stuck her heels into the pony.

"Halt, please! Right now! Whoa!"

Mike stopped. Before Mary could urge him on again, Henry Zelinski was in front of them, blocking the way. He took hold of the pony's rein.

"Mary, you have been granted the gift of a very special horse. Believe me, a mare such as yours comes along once in a lifetime, if a rider is lucky. *You* have an obligation to your horse to be the best rider you can be—"

"That's what I try to do, but—"

"Listen! Please, be quiet. I will teach you how to ride."

"I know how to ride! I've been riding all my life. And there's nothing wrong with Colleen, either. She's a good horse. She does whatever I ask her to do. Thank you, Mr. Zee, but me and Colleen are doing just fine."

"All right, then—if you are determined to remain ignorant, so be it." Henry Zelinski let go of Mike's rein. He spun on the heel of his tall riding boot and stalked away into the house.

Mary looked over at Dorothy standing nearby. The woman gave Mary a sad smile. "Goodbye now, Mary. Thank you for the visit." She hurried after her husband.

Drumming her heels against her pony's sides, Mary galloped home.

6

"I don't know what you're trying to do with that mare, but whatever it is, you'd better quit. She's not learning anything when she's all riled up like that."

Mary hadn't noticed her father leaning against a fence post. She'd been too intent on trying to get Colleen to do the same slow, high-stepping trot she'd seen Dorothy and Henry Zelinski's horses perform. Colleen shook her head angrily at the pressure of the bit in her mouth. She tried to halt but Mary's calves squeezed hard into her sides, urging her on. Confused by the conflicting signals—*stop* and *go*—the mare stiffened her spine.

"I'm telling you: she's had enough," warned Dad. "You'd better leave off before—aw, heck! You okay?"

"I'm fine," muttered Mary. She pushed herself to her feet, more surprised than hurt. Colleen had never bucked before, not ever.

Dad ducked through the fence. "Well, you look like you're still in one piece. Are you hurting real bad anywhere?"

"No, just a bit bruised." She dusted the seat of her jeans. "Look at her run."

Side by side they watched Colleen race around the perimeter of the small field, kicking up her heels. Mama cows with late babies beside them scattered to the far side.

"She's got some go, that mare," observed Dad. "It might be a while before she'll let you catch her again."

"I can't let her get away with bucking me off."

"She didn't throw you to have her own way. You got tossed because she didn't understand what you were asking her to do and you kept asking. Whose fault is that?"

Mary stabbed the grass with her boot. "Mine."

"You're darn right it is. A cold-blooded horse, you ask too much of him and he'll close right down, shut you right out as if nothing was happening to him, but a hot horse like your mare, well, she doesn't know how to quit. She'll keep on trying until she can't take any more. Then she'll blow up, like Colleen just did."

"So how am I supposed to train her to do anything?"

"You got to know when to ask and when to back off. As soon as she gives you a little bit of what you're wanting, quit asking. Let her have a break. Mary, you know all this. I shouldn't be having to tell you again."

"Yeah, yeah, it's just that...she wasn't doing what I asked at all, not even a little bit. So how was I supposed to stop asking?"

"What were you asking her to do, anyway?"

"It's called piaffe. It's kind of like trotting in one spot."

Dad rubbed at his jaw. "Like a circus trick, eh?"

"No, it's different than that. It's part of something called dressage. It's supposed to make your horse more obedient."

"Hmm." He was quiet with his own thoughts for some time. Colleen slowed to a prancing jog, close by the cows and calves. A white-face shook her head, warning the mare to keep back from her calf. Colleen scooted off and made another circuit of the pasture.

Dad chuckled. "More obedient, huh?"

"That's what Mr. Zelinski said."

"Hmm. Well, I heard he did some kind of fancy horse training."

Colleen reached the far corner of the field. She skidded to a stop and stood with her head held high, staring out across the pastures and orchards to the blue mountains beyond. Her hindquarters crouched down. Mary was sure the golden mare was about to jump the fence, but she suddenly swung around and trotted in place, her flaxen tail arched and her hooves lifting high, a slow, measured half beat between each step.

"There! There, look, she's doing it! That's piaffe."

"That's just playing around. Lots of horses prance around like that when they're feeling good. Never knew there was a special name for it." Dad settled his hat lower on his head. "Nice to see a horse doing that kind of thing all on her own. Not sure it's worth getting bucked off for. Just my opinion."

Mary nodded to show she'd heard. Most of what she knew about horses had come from her father. The rest had been taught to her by the horses themselves. "They're the best teachers," Dad always said. "If you're willing to pay attention and learn."

She'd seen her father do a lot with horses over the years. Everyone on the ranch said he was the best at starting colts, bringing them along with such skill and patience that there was never a spook in them or a hump under the saddle. From time to time he took on horses that other so-called riders had spoiled, fixing them up so whatever bad acting they'd taken on to avoid being ridden—balking, bucking, nipping—was given up, and they were honest, hard-working partners again.

There was no doubt Donny Inglis was a good horseman. But she'd never seen him ride a horse so it was dancing.

"She's coming back to you now," said Dad. Colleen was striding low-headed across the grass toward them. Mary moved to meet her. She pressed her face against the thin streak of white in the middle of the mare's head.

"I'm sorry. Forgive me."

Colleen breathed out a long, fluttering sigh. She dropped her head lower, letting the girl wrap her arms around her flat, bony cheeks. Mary's heart stung at the trust the horse gave her. She closed her eyes and mirrored the mare's deep breaths with her own.

After a time, Colleen shifted restlessly. Mary let go. Taking a handful of silver mane, she swung up onto the mare's back. The long June dusk was easing into a warm night lit by a half moon. Dad was strolling back to the house. Knotting the slack in the reins, Mary let them hang loose on Colleen's neck.

"Let's go," she whispered. "Let's just go."

She only had to chirp and Colleen was flying across the field. Mary set her eye on the cattle feeder built into the fenceline. As surely as if she'd been steering Colleen with hands and legs, the mare galloped at the solid wood bunk. Three strides away, two, one and they were in the air, soaring out of the field over the feeder. For a few precious moments they were completely and absolutely free of everything, even the earth.

Colleen touched down on the ranch road. Of her own accord she turned right, loping easily along the packed dirt road. Bit by bit it began to climb and then they were in the trees, the dark forest embracing them, hiding them from the ranch and bringing them into a world of their very own.

The road bent in a hairpin turn and came out onto a long grassy bench straddling the mountainside. Colleen lifted her head, alert to the shadows at the far end of the natural meadow. She whickered softly. The shadows shifted, dark shapes emerging and moving toward them. Mary caught her breath as the shapes formed into horses, nickering soft greetings to her mare.

The wild herd. She'd never come upon them so close to the ranch before. There was the old chestnut mare with the blazed face, cautiously approaching to breathe in Mary's human scent. Every member of the small band stood on alert, head high and ears forward. With a sigh, the old mare dropped her head and resumed grazing, one ear cocked in Mary's direction. The other horses soon went back to eating as well.

"It's okay, I won't hurt you." Mary kept her voice low and soft.

One or two horses raised their heads at the sound, but the rest of the herd kept on eating, undisturbed. Mary smiled to herself, pleased. They were getting used to the sound of her voice. They were accepting her.

She made out the palomino mare deeper in the shadows of the trees. Last time she'd seen her, a couple of months ago, the young mare had been big bellied with foal, but now...yes, there it was, a sturdy foal pressed close to her side. It was pale coloured, maybe another palomino like its mama. Mary wanted to ride closer and see, but she held back. She'd learned from experience that if she and Colleen came too near, the band would slip off into the forest.

"Look, Colleen, do you see the baby? A niece or a nephew for you, eh?" She liked to think the palomino mare shared Colleen's sire. After all, their rare golden colouring with the silver mane and tail had to come from somewhere.

She realized the distance between Colleen and the band had grown. The bench meadow was emptying, the wild horses melting away between the trees, moving on to other grazing. Of her own accord, Colleen turned around and headed down the mountain.

Mary gave the mare her head. She lay on her back atop the mare, watching the stars glitter in the night sky.

When they reached home and Colleen was safely tucked away in her pasture, strong teeth ripping at the sweet grass, Mary went inside the house and tugged off her boots. She was halfway up the stairs to her room when Dad called her back.

"Something here for you." He pushed a book across the kitchen table. "Mrs. Zelinski dropped it off."

Mary eyed the book suspiciously. "What is it?"

He gave the book another shove. "See for yourself. Come on, Mary, it's not going to bite."

Mary picked up the book. It was a scrapbook, thick with photos and newspaper clippings. "What's this for?"

"I guess she wants you to have a look through."

Mary peeked inside the cover. Stuck to the first page was the photo of a young boy, twelve or thirteen, grinning beside a pinto pony. She recognized Henry Zelinski. Mary dropped the book on the table. "What do I need to look at this for?"

Her father didn't reply. Instead, he pulled the scrapbook closer and began leafing through the pages, pausing every so often to read a caption or study a picture.

Mary marched upstairs, washed and put on her pyjamas. She crawled into bed and lay there, sleepless. She leaned over the side of her bed and pulled out a cardboard shoebox. Curled inside was a magazine. She sat up and the magazine fell open to the centre spread.

She hardly needed the moonlight to read the caption: *Pacific National Exhibition.* She traced her finger down the page, past the photographs of prize dairy cows and champion roosters, to a picture of a dark horse rearing up to leap over a huge wall. In the next photo a horse stood at attention, noble head high, while his smiling rider, a lean-faced man in a black hunt cap, accepted a trophy. In the background of both photos the stands were packed with people, a sea of blurry faces.

Mary could close her eyes and recall every detail of that pair of photographs. Two pictures—they were all she had to nourish her dream.

Until now. Mary looked up. Her room was small, her bed close to the window. She could see Colleen grazing, a pale, ghostly figure in the dark. Even as Mary watched her, the mare lifted her head and stared up at the girl's window.

Mary pushed the bedcovers aside and went to the window. She lifted out the screen and leaned over the sill. "What is it?"

Colleen continued to stare up at her. The mare shook her head, silver mane spinning like stardust in the night, and stamped her foot.

Mary had the uncanny sense that her horse was trying to tell her something. She couldn't figure out what it might be. Perhaps if she could clear her mind...but all she could think of was the scrapbook Dorothy Zelinski had brought to the house. What was in it that she wanted Mary to see?

Curiosity won out. Mary crept downstairs and found the scrapbook. Bringing it upstairs, she turned on her bedside lamp and sat cross-legged under her blankets. Slowly she turned over the first page.

Later, much later, she understood that her first instinct to shy away from Henry Zelinski's scrapbook had been the right one. With every page she turned, the yearning grew in her. Photo after photo of shining horses stretching over tall fences; clipping after clipping relating the feats of courage and agility— if she hadn't opened the book, if she hadn't known, this restless longing might never have hatched. But she had and it did and it was growing so fast and so huge it consumed every thought, every feeling in her, until it was all she was.

Dizzy with fatigue, she fell back on her pillows, the scrapbook beside her, the lamp still glowing. Her eyelids fell shut but scene after scene played out in her mind, horse after horse leaping into the air over enormous obstacles. Every detail was as clear as if she'd been wide awake. She could see the bunch of the animal's muscles, hear it grunt as it pushed off the ground. The rider's polished boots gleamed, the coattails fluttered. But the face under the black velvet cap brim was not Henry Zelinski's.

It was hers.

7

Henry Zelinski jumped when he turned to find Mary standing in the open doorway of the barn. "What are you doing there?"

"I...I'm sorry." Mary couldn't help shrinking away from his glare. "I didn't mean to interrupt. I'll go."

"No, don't!" Dorothy's head popped out of one of the stalls. "Henry, you must stop barking at people. It puts them off."

"The girl keeps appearing out of nowhere, like a ghost," he complained. "It's very unsettling."

"I did go to the house first," Mary explained. "There was no one there."

"Come over here, dear, so we can talk while I finish doing up Valiant."

Mary edged past Henry to the stall where Dorothy rolled a long white bandage over a quilt wrapped around the horse's lower leg. Two of his legs were already encased in bandages.

"Is he hurt?" she asked.

Dorothy shook her head. "He's not injured, just old and stiff. The bandages help keep his legs warm. Henry should be wrapping his own horse but, frankly,

I'm better at it." She winked at Mary. "Here, would you like to try?"

Nodding, Mary crouched down next to Dorothy. Following her instructions, she wrapped a large padded square of quilted cotton around Valiant's leg from the bottom of his knee down.

"Now, make sure any wrinkles are smoothed away. Like this." Deftly, Dorothy's fingers smoothed away a crease. "Take that rolled-up bandage—that's the one—fit the end under the edge of the quilt close to the top and roll it around the leg. Make sure you keep it nice and snug."

"Not too tight or you'll cause a bowed tendon," said Henry.

"Too loose and the bandage will simply fall off," continued his wife. "You're doing fine, Mary, just fine. You're getting it nice and even. Well done, you."

"When you reach the end, tie it off, but be sure...that's right, on the outside of the leg," said Henry. "Not bad. Not bad at all for a first attempt."

Hunkered down beside Mary, Dorothy bumped her shoulder against the girl's and grinned. "Don't let all that praise go to your head."

They stood up and leaned against the stall wall, admiring the glossy, dark bay horse before them. "He's still a good-looking fellow, even at nineteen, isn't he, Mary?"

Mary's eyes travelled over the tall rangy horse, noting the satin coat and the well-toned muscling underneath;

the silky mane and tail, neatly trimmed and meticulously combed; the bright, intelligent eyes and the tapered ears. Now that she was looking for it, she saw a deepening in the hollows above the eyes and a slackening in the spine just behind the withers. She reached out her hand and the horse gently sniffed her palm.

"And this is Vega," said Dorothy, moving to the next stall. "You saw me riding her the other day."

Mary stroked the brown neck. "Hello, you." Vega's dark eyes regarded her kindly.

"She's a sweetie, a real pet." Dorothy lowered her voice. "We'd hoped she might be the one, she's got the ability, but she's just not dependable. The littlest things put her right off her game."

Henry came up beside them. "So, Mary, is there a reason for your visit this evening?"

"Well, I..." Where had her prepared speech gone?

"Don't mutter! If you've got something to say, speak up and say it," growled Henry.

"Henry, perhaps Mary just came for a friendly visit," said Dorothy.

"No, that's not why I'm here." Mary squared her shoulders. "Will you teach me? Like you said you would. About riding and other stuff, like this bandaging."

"I believe the 'other stuff' you're referring to is what horsemen know as stable management. What do you want to learn about riding, Mary?"

"Everything. Everything there is to know about riding and horses and how to look after them."

Henry's eyes narrowed. "Everything? I suppose you think you can learn it all in a few weeks."

"No, no, there's so much I don't know. It'll take a long time, years and years. And you don't have to tell me it'll be hard work. That much I do know. Hard work doesn't scare me, not one bit. The only thing that scares me is…"

"What? What scares you? Go on, tell me."

"Missing this chance. That's what scares me. 'Cause I might not get another one, not living way out here on this ranch. My dad, he knows lots about horses, but he wasn't in any cavalry, not like your father, so he can't help me. And there's no one else. Before, it didn't matter because I didn't know there was more, but now that I do know, well, I can't just *un*know. It just won't leave me alone. I have to do something, I have to learn."

Henry Zelinski's expression was unchanged. He wasn't going to help her.

"Please, there is no one else," she pleaded. "No one but you."

"All right. I'll do it."

"You will? Really?"

"Yes, of course I will. I said I would, didn't I? If you're ready to learn, I'll teach you."

"When can I come? School's done for the summer so I can come anytime. Except for when I'm needed on the ranch."

"You could begin right now if you had your mare with you," said Dorothy.

"Oh, but I do." Mary stepped out the barn door and whistled. A moment later, Colleen appeared.

"Where's her bridle?" asked Henry.

"At home. I ride her in a halter when I'm just riding around."

Dorothy took her by the arm and led her down the alley of the barn. "Come on, Mary, I've got a pair of boots and a hard hat in the tack room that I think will fit you."

"Oh, but I don't need—"

"Oh, but you do. You absolutely do need to wear a hard hat."

Mary stopped protesting when she saw the tall leather boots Dorothy brought out of a wooden trunk.

"You'll never get them on over your jeans. Here, try these." She pulled out a pair of riding breeches, wide legged at the top but close fitting from the knee down.

The breeches were surprisingly comfortable, but the boots, once she tugged them on with the help of boot pulls, were stiff and tight on her ankles and calves. "I don't like them. I don't want to wear them." She sat on the tack trunk, lifted one foot onto the other knee and began to pull.

"Mary, please leave them on. Give yourself some time to get used to them. Here, try this on for size." Dorothy held out a black velvet-covered cap with a small brim.

Mary blinked at the hard hat. Then, slowly, reverently, she settled it on her head.

"How does that feel? Too tight? Too loose? Nod your head; it should stay in place."

"It feels fine," she replied, dipping her head up and down.

"Stand up, let's have a look at you. Very nice, Mary. Riding clothes suit you. Come on now, we don't want to keep Henry waiting."

Clomping down the alley in the boots, she followed Dorothy outside. Henry stood holding Colleen. The mare now wore a flat jumping saddle and a gleaming leather bridle with a snaffle bit.

"She doesn't need that saddle," said Mary. "I don't ride her in one."

"She has been saddled before, hasn't she?" asked Henry.

"Oh, yes, Dad used a stock saddle on her when he started her. But—"

"Then when you ride for me you will use a saddle. It is essential if you are going to learn to ride properly. And a jumping saddle is required in competition."

"Competition?" echoed Mary. "You mean horse shows?"

"Yes, I do."

"Mary may not be interested in competing, Henry, not everyone is. She is a young lady, after all," said Dorothy.

"But I do want to jump in horse shows! I really, truly do."

"Is that so? Do you want it enough to practise every day, rain or shine?"

"Yes, yes, of course."

"Will you ignore bruises and blisters and aching muscles? When you are sick to your stomach with nerves, will you put aside your fear so no one, not even your horse, realizes you are anything but supremely confident? When everyone around you says you can't, will you still believe *you can*?"

Mary said nothing, her heart thudding in confusion. She didn't understand: Henry Zelinski had gone from offering to teach her and Colleen to doing his best to discourage her. Well, he could rant and rave all he wanted; he wasn't going to scare her off jumping. She lifted her chin and pulled her spine tall and straight. "I can do it."

"Oh, really? Because they'll say you can't. They'll tell you you're not strong enough, not determined enough, not *tough* enough to ride up there with the best in the country—all because you're a girl. That's the attitude we're up against. That's why I'm asking you, Mary: do you want this more than anything else?"

"Oh, yes. More than anything in the world."

"Then we'll begin right now."

8

"Again," said Henry.

Mary badly wanted to shake her head, but she was just too exhausted. Her legs, hanging down the flaps of the borrowed jumping saddle, were as wobbly as jelly. Henry had slid the stirrup leathers off their bars at the beginning of the lesson. Without stirrups to set her feet in, all that was keeping her on top of the smooth leather was her strength and balance. And with her muscles feeling so weary, she wasn't going to be able to rely on strength much longer.

At least the churned-up dirt in the corral would be soft when she hit it. She knew that from bitter experience. In the three weeks she'd been riding under Henry Zelinski's instruction, she'd fallen off many times. The record was five falls in one lesson, but that was in the early days. Lately, she'd only come off once or twice a session. *That* was an improvement, one of the few she seemed to have made, and she'd never been hurt. Sometimes she even landed on her feet.

"Henry, darling, maybe you should call it a day," suggested Dorothy, sitting atop the corral fence.

"You've been drilling Mary for nearly an hour now. This isn't military school, after all."

"The very best horsemen in the world have come out of military schools. That's where my father learned, and that's how he taught me."

"But Mary isn't a young officer in training. She's a *girl*."

"Ah, so she is weak! She has no fortitude, no grit! No wonder they won't allow women to jump in the Olympic Games. They're too soft and fragile." He sighed, shaking his head sadly. "Mary, put your horse away. That's all for today."

"Oh, no, it's not." Mary picked up the knotted reins and steered Colleen around the short end of the corral. Before them a row of low jumps had been set close together. She dropped the reins onto the mare's neck, held her arms straight out from her sides and, now without stirrups or reins, sent the mare to the jumps in a canter.

Hop, hop, hop. Colleen skipped neatly over the jumps, Mary following her movements in perfect balance and harmony.

"Very good," shouted Henry after the last jump. "That's very good."

Very good—twice? Mary gaped at him, shocked by the praise. "But I didn't do anything."

"Ah, here"—Henry tapped his forehead—"you did not. But in here"—he pressed his fist to the centre of his chest—"you went with the horse. This part knows how to do this better. You *feel* the riding. Then, and only then, the horse and rider become as one. This is what we have been trying for. Understand?"

Mary nodded enthusiastically.

"Good. Now, do it again."

"Dad, does Mr. Zelinski do a good job of running the ranch?" Mary asked. Sitting on the steps of the veranda in the cool of the evening, she looked up at her father leaning back in the old rocker, one leg hooked over the arm.

"Well, now, it's early days yet, but it looks like he's going to work out just fine. What do you think, Tom?"

Mary's older brother joined Mary on the steps. "Mr. Zee? He's okay. At first the men weren't too sure about him because of the way he acts..."

"Like he's in the army!" giggled Mary.

"Yeah, that's it. But he's fair and he keeps his word, and that goes a long way with me and the rest of the guys."

"He's willing to listen to a man," said Dad. "That's what I like about him."

"There's something else I want to know: how come there aren't any women working on the ranch?" Mary asked.

"Who says there aren't? Every woman on this spread works hard cooking and cleaning and sewing for their families."

"I mean doing *ranch* work."

"Well, I suppose because we've never had a girl come looking for a job as a ranch hand."

"Because they can't do the work?"

"They sure as heck can! Back when the war was on and most of the men were gone, it was the women that kept the farms and ranches going. They did a fine job of it, too. Calving and roping and branding—they did it all. *And* raised the children."

"So a woman can do anything a man can?"

"Pretty much. Sometimes it doesn't seem like she can, because a woman'll go about things differently than a man."

"What do you mean?"

"Well, a woman doesn't have the strength a man has, that's just a fact. But that doesn't mean she's helpless. In my experience, when a gal wants to get something done, she'll find a way to get things working in her favour without any need for brute strength. That's why a horse'll act so kind and gentle for a lady rider, because she doesn't try to outmuscle it, the way a lot of men will. She'll get that animal doing what she wants by persuasion, not force." The rocker creaked as Dad tipped back and forth. "Your mama could sweet-talk a horse into doing just about anything."

Mary held her tongue, hoping her father would say more about her mother, but that was all. She knew it was useless to push him to talk. The many times she'd tried, he'd suddenly come up with something that needed doing right away and would be out of the house and gone.

"What's this all about, anyway?" he asked.

"Nothing. I've got to go check the horses' water tub." She got up and was away before he could say another word.

* * *

"Easy, easy! That is too much!" shouted Henry as Valiant lashed out a hind leg in protest.

"But he won't do it! He won't canter," said Mary. She was struggling to sit the big bay's trot, but he was rushing around the training corral, his back so tense she was sure he was trying to bounce her right out of the saddle.

"Walk now!"

Valiant responded so quickly, Mary knew he was obeying Henry's voice and not her aids. She didn't care. She was so frustrated by the obstinacy of the animal underneath, she was ready to quit. This wasn't what she'd expected when Henry had told her that riding his old campaigner would give her the chance to feel what it was like to be on a highly trained horse.

"He will not canter because you are not asking properly," explained Henry.

"I am! Inside leg at the girth, outside leg behind— I'm doing everything the right way."

"Plainly you are not, or the horse would canter. Here, I'll show you."

Mary slid down out of Valiant's saddle. Ignoring the stirrup, Henry vaulted up onto the horse's back. He crossed the stirrups in front of the saddle and picked up the reins. Immediately, the bay was alert, poised and waiting for his rider's requests.

"See, like this." From a standstill, Valiant shifted into canter, floating softly over the ground. He turned across the middle of the corral and switched forelegs to lead with his left. Two strides later he changed back to his right. Left, right, left, right—he swapped leads every stride in perfect rhythm, skipping to the beat of a merry dance.

Mary crossed her arms and watched with sullen admiration.

Then she saw it, the lightest brush of the leg, just back of the girth. There it was again. She realized Henry wasn't showing off but demonstrating to her how to apply the aid. Her arms fell as she leaned forward, squinting to see more clearly. Barely a nudge, but instantly understood by the horse.

"Can I try again?"

"Of course." Henry brought Valiant to a halt and dismounted. Only a few minutes later he held up his hands and tapped them together to mime applause. "You have it!"

Mary was riding on air. Valiant carried her so gently she could hardly feel his hooves hitting the earth.

There was nothing for her to do but follow his rocking motion. After all the strain and struggle, this was so easy. She could ride like this forever.

"Now, come across on the diagonal. Ask for the other lead, gently, gently, just shift your...that's it! You have got it. And again."

Valiant was dancing underneath her. No, he was dancing with her. She could feel his delight in the expression of his own grace and power. He was giving all that she asked for and enjoying the partnership.

All too soon Henry said, "That is enough for today."

Back on the ground, Mary lifted the reins over Valiant's head to lead him back to the barn. The bay hooked his head over her shoulder and pulled her close.

"Valiant," she protested, "what on earth?" She squirmed to get away but the horse pressed harder, holding her tight to his chest. Mary stood still. She leaned against Valiant, absorbing the steady rhythm of his breathing, the giant thudding of his great heart. After long, precious moments he took his head away. She stepped back and looked into his dark eyes and recognized trust.

You understood.

She nodded. *I did. Thank you.*

Valiant tugged gently at the reins. Side by side, they walked back to the barn.

* * *

"That's good, very good," Henry said a week later as Colleen came quietly to a walk from canter. Not a pull at the bit or a shake of the head. Mary grinned, pleased with her horse and herself. Now that Colleen was learning how to respond to the subtle nuances of pressure from the rider's hands and legs, she was becoming much more relaxed and cooperative. They were growing together in harmony.

Colleen was changing in other ways as well. Her back was growing stronger, the muscles in her neck and quarters becoming firm and well defined. Mary noticed her own strength was increasing, and her stamina, too. She rarely lost her balance, and her reflexes were quick and precise. At the end of a training session she was tired, but not exhausted—not bone-weary, as she'd been the first few weeks.

"Now we will jump."

Mary turned Colleen to put her on track to the row of low jumps.

"No, not here." Henry opened the corral gate. "We'll go to the jumping field. It's time for you to try something new."

The jumping field was a corner of a nearby pasture. Brightly painted striped poles sat on top of upturned oil drums, bales of old straw had been stacked to form a tall wall, and a ditch had been dug by hand. There was even a picnic table complete with straw-stuffed dummies propped up on the benches and dressed in ranch clothes, cowboy hats and polka-dotted neckerchiefs.

Henry surveyed the jumping course. "Dorothy, you're a genius. Look what you have created. Go on, Mary, take your horse around and let her have a look."

Colleen barely flapped an ear at the makeshift jumps. Guided by Mary, she trotted, then cantered around and between the obstacles while Henry and Dorothy watched from the middle of the course. After a few minutes, Henry called her over. He pointed out a track over six jumps. "All right, then, give it a go."

Mary picked up the reins, asked Colleen to canter and turned her toward the first jump of their first ever show jumping course.

The mare's ears snapped forward as she sighted the strange obstacle in their path. Mary squeezed her calves, urging her on. She could feel her horse's body coiling into a spring. Then they were off the ground and flying over the double rails. Mary watched as the striped poles passed underneath them in a blur. Colleen dropped down to earth again, her eyes fixed on the next fence straight ahead, tugging at the bit in her eagerness to get to it.

Up and over and around a turn to the third. Then the fourth, and after it, only two strides away, another set of double rails on oil drums. Colleen checked, surprised by the close distance between the jumps. Somehow, she compressed her long stride to fit and gave a mighty leap over the wide jump. She landed with a shake of her head, kicking up her heels.

Thrown onto the mare's neck, Mary laughed out loud and pushed herself back into position. She looked over her shoulder for the sixth jump, the final challenge, the picnic table. Colleen's buck had taken them past the turn that would have brought them right over the centre of the obstacle.

"Come on, Colleen!" Mary turned hard, the mare skidding around her own body like a barrel racer. They were coming at the jump on an angle, but she didn't know what else to do. Henry had told her the only thing that mattered was getting over the jump without knocking it down.

The mare's head came up, her attention held by the surprising obstacle in her path. Coming at this pace, the straw dummies in their hats and plaid shirts looked like real people. Mary felt a rare moment of doubt. Would her mare jump?

Yes, yes, she would! There was no hesitation in Colleen's stride. With the bold courage that had carried them over five-foot gates and a sports car, she sprang into the air, soaring so high above the picnic table that Mary could see the crowns of the cowboy hats on the dummies below. She felt light-headed with joy, dizzy with pride in her brave, marvellous horse. When Colleen's front hooves set down, she threw her arms around the mare's neck, hugging her tight while the palomino raced across the field.

She let her run halfway around the field before gently bringing her down to a walk. Colleen was proud and excited, jigging sideways as they headed back over the grass.

Henry Zelinski was running toward them. "Thank goodness you got her pulled up. You're okay?"

"Yes, of course. I just let her have her head because she jumped so well."

Dorothy caught up. "What happened? Did she run away with you?"

"Oh, no, I let her run. It was her reward."

"I see," puffed Dorothy. "Perhaps in the future you might try a lump of sugar instead of a headlong gallop."

"She jumped pretty good, didn't she?" Mary smoothed her mare's ruffled mane.

"Pretty good?" repeated Henry. "She was absolutely magnificent, that's what she was. She's a natural! She went around that course like she's jumped it a hundred times. What a wonderful, wonderful horse!"

Mary stared down at him as he patted Colleen's neck over and over. She'd never seen Henry like this, so excited and happy.

Dorothy caught her eye and winked. "She could go anywhere and win. The Royal Winter Fair, the Garden, anywhere! Mary, what's the matter? What's wrong?"

Mary's own smile had fallen away as she remembered the last occasion there had been talk of Colleen at all the big horse shows. She shook her head. "I don't want to lose her."

"What are you talking about?" Henry said. "Nobody's going to take her away from you. *You* would ride her. I'll teach you, train you both, but you will be her rider."

"Really? You'd really do that?"

"Yes, I would. Many people have helped me along the way. Now I will help you, and one day, when you have years and years of experience, you will pass what you've learned along to someone else."

Mary nodded. "I will. I promise I will. But—"

"Another but?"

"What about school? And money. We haven't got very much, you know."

Henry waved aside her concerns. "All that can be worked out. What matters is you have the horse and you have the desire. Mary, you're on your way."

9

"The Pacific National Exhibition," repeated Dad. "You want Mary to enter her horse in the jumping at the PNE."

"Yes, that's what I said." Henry pushed a booklet across the table to him. "Here's the prize list. I've checked the classes Mary will go in. You need to sign the entry form as her guardian because she's under eighteen."

"The PNE is in Vancouver. That's a big city," said Tom.

Dad nodded. "It's a long way from Vernon." He shifted on the high-backed dining chair, trying to get comfortable. He looked around the room, taking in the ornate chandelier overhead, the dark panelled walls, the heavy velvet curtains at the narrow windows and the surface of the long table. The old boss and his wife hadn't invited the ranch employees to the big house very often, and certainly not for supper. "That's nine or ten hours of travelling."

"Yes, it will take a day to drive the horses down there," said Henry.

"Horses?"

"I'm entering one of my horses. Of course, with

Mary and her Colleen as competition, I don't think we have much of a chance, but we'll do our best." Henry gave Dad a smile that wasn't returned.

Mary's heart sank. This wasn't going well. Dorothy caught her eye and winked.

"Hold your horses, Mr. Zelinski. Nothing's been decided," Dad began.

Dorothy jumped up, her chair scraping against the hardwood floor. "It's awfully warm in here, don't you think? Let's go sit out on the veranda. There's a pot of tea and a chocolate cake waiting for us in the kitchen. Tom, would you mind helping me carry things?"

"Sure, Mrs. Zee."

"Henry, why don't you and Mr. Inglis head out to the veranda."

"Just Donny, ma'am."

"Then Donny it is. Mary, come and help your brother and me."

Mary hurried out of the room after Dorothy. "He's not going to let me go in the horse show," she whispered.

"Give him time, Mary. He has to get used to the idea. And this will help sweeten him up." With a flourish, Dorothy uncovered a double-layer cake with chocolate icing.

"It's very nice to stay in a hotel, of course, but Henry and I prefer to be closer to our horses. Many of the competitors do. We fix up a spare stall as a sleeping room, set up a couple of cots…It's really very comfortable. Tom, please have another slice of cake," said Dorothy.

"Well, ma'am, I've already had two."

"You're a hard-working young man, that's what Henry tells me. I'm sure you can fit in another piece."

Sheepishly, Tom held out his plate.

"Donny, how about you?"

"I'm fine, ma'am. That sure was good cake."

"I'm pleased you enjoyed it. Now, what else is there to talk about?" Dorothy looked brightly around her.

Dad's hand started to reach up for his hat before he remembered it was on the floor beside him. He rubbed at his chin instead. "Well, I imagine it costs something to go into this jumping contest."

"Oh, yes, the entry fees. One last chance for cake, everyone. No? Mary, would you please take the cake into the kitchen and cover it up so it doesn't get stale. Thank you. You've done a fine job raising your daughter, Donny. You must be so proud of her."

"I am. Now about those entry fees."

In the kitchen, Mary hurriedly set the cake under a glass dome. She strained her ears to hear the conversation outside.

"Donny, I can tell you're the sort of man who respects hard work and achievement," Dorothy was saying.

"That's true, I do," Dad agreed.

Mary stood inside the kitchen door, listening.

"Mary has learned a lot from you. I've never seen a young lady work as hard as your daughter. Henry is amazed at how quickly she's progressed with her mare. Now, we believe such hard work should be rewarded, so Henry and I would like to cover the cost of Mary's entry fees."

"No, Mrs. Zelinski, I can't let you do that. This family has never taken handouts and we're not starting now."

"But, Donny, we just want to help. Mary is such a good rider, and her horse has so much ability. She deserves this opportunity to show just how good they are!"

"She's young and so's the mare. There'll be other chances for them to show off." Dad leaned over and picked up his hat. "Mrs. Zee, Mister, thank you for the meal and the hospitality." He got to his feet.

"You're welcome, Donny." Henry rose and shook hands.

Tom stood up, hat in hand. "I've got a suggestion to make."

"What is it, Tom?" asked Dorothy.

"Mary could earn the money to pay her own entry fees. She's fourteen now, getting close to fifteen—it's time she started paying her own way."

"How would she do that?" asked Dad.

"By working, just like the rest of us do."

"She could help me in the house," said Dorothy. "Dusting, sweeping, cleaning windows, that sort of thing. I could find lots for her to do."

"Well, ma'am, I was thinking more along the lines of actual ranch work. Haying's going to start real soon. We can use every hand we can get."

Dad shook his head. "Your sister's a strong girl, but she'd have a hard time keeping up with the men."

"I'm not talking about pitching hay. Mary could drive the tractor pulling the hay sloop around the field while the men load it."

"Except with haying about to start any day now, there's no time to teach her how to drive a tractor."

"Oh, she doesn't need to be taught. She already knows." Tom couldn't hide his grin. "I showed her how two years ago when you had me doing the very same job. Heck, Mary's been driving a tractor since she was twelve. Right, sis?"

He stuck his head inside the door, and Mary realized he'd known she was there all along. She stepped outside.

"I can do it, Dad. I'll work really hard and pay my way. Just let me go, please? I really want to do this. It's not about showing off, it's about..." She paused, thinking back to what Mr. Zee had told her about competition. "It's about giving everything you have to do your very best."

Dad twirled his hat by the brim, around and around. He watched the woven straw revolve as if he were mesmerized. His shoulders began to shake.

Tom put a hand on their father's shoulder. "Hey, you all right?"

"You bet I am." He looked up and they realized he was laughing. "Driving the tractor since she was twelve. That's my girl. My Miss Mary."

"So, can I go?"

Dad slung his arm around her shoulders. "You've got my permission. But there's one condition: you're not going by yourself."

"We'll take care of her, Donny, don't you worry," said Dorothy.

"I'm sure you will. But if Mr. Zee can spare him from the ranch, I'd like her big brother to go too."

"Donny, we'll work something out. We'll make it happen," said Henry.

"Oh, Dad!" Mary hugged her father, then her brother. "Tom, can you believe it? We're going to the PNE!"

10

The Zelinskis' car led the way through the busy streets. Tom was silent as he drove the big truck through the heavy traffic, his eyes fixed on the vehicle ahead. A car cut in front of the truck and he braked sharply to avoid hitting it. The truck rocked as the horses scrambled to regain their balance. Mary twisted in her seat, peering through the slits into the box.

"Everything okay?" asked Tom, shifting gears.

"Looks like it. It's hard to see much." Mary let out her breath. "Whew, that was close."

"Sure was. Everything's close down here. Too close."

He was right. Cars, buses, delivery vans and trucks flowed up and down the streets like a debris-filled river during spring runoff. People hurried past one another on the sidewalks, and the buildings were crowded tight together, reaching high into the sky to block out the sun. There was so much of everything.

"They're turning," Mary said. "At the next corner. They're going right."

"I see them." Tom eased the truck to a slower speed and followed the Zelinskis' right turn at the intersection.

And there it was, acres and acres of parkland and massive buildings, the biggest Mary had ever seen. She spotted a Ferris wheel and caught a glimpse of a huge, roofed grandstand and a racetrack. Tom switched lanes and turned in to the grounds, stopping behind the Zelinskis' car at a tiny hut. Henry had his window rolled down and was leaning out the window to speak with the security guard in the hut. The man stepped out, gesturing directions with his hand in the air. Henry nodded and waved his thanks, and the convoy rolled on.

They unloaded the horses using a ramp at the cattle barn. Leading Colleen to her stable in the Livestock Pavilion, Mary saw other horses arriving. They had travelled in vans and horse trailers and unloaded on attached ramps. One groom jogged another with his elbow, pointing to the cattle truck. Both men chuckled and shook their heads.

Mary ducked her head and looked around. Henry was leading Vega as proudly as if he'd just unloaded her from a deluxe six-horse van. Perhaps he hadn't noticed the men laughing.

But he had. He winked and said softly, "Remember, he who laughs last laughs best."

They walked the two horses for ten minutes to help ease any stiffness from the long journey. Colleen's head was high, taking in the strange sights and scents. She tossed her head and pranced a little.

"I know, it's exciting to be here," Mary said to her.

She felt like prancing herself. The air around them was charged with excitement.

Dorothy found their stalls, and they led the horses deep into the building. The alleys were narrow and crowded. Shrill whinnies echoed off the walls and roof of the stable area, punctuated by the lowing of cattle and bleating of sheep nearby. Mary wondered how her horse would get any rest with all this hubbub and bustle.

"Right here." Dorothy stopped at the three stalls assigned to them. Two were bedded with straw. "The third one's for our tack."

"That's where we'll bed down, Tom," said Henry.

"Fine with me."

While Mary and Dorothy removed the mares' shipping bandages and sheets, the men found wheelbarrows and unloaded feed and gear. Soon the horses were settled with hay and fresh water. The trunks of riding equipment, the sleeping cots, the stable tools, and suitcases with riding clothes and the men's everyday clothes were neatly arranged in the third stall. Dorothy and Mary tied a blanket across the front of the stall for privacy.

Tom and Henry went to clean horse droppings out of the truck box. Then they would move it to the assigned parking lot, spread a tarp on the floor and set up cots for Mary and Dorothy to sleep on.

"We won't be the only ones camping out," Dorothy assured Mary. "There'll be lots of others. People want to be close by so they can check on their animals." She led the way through the aisles into the arena. "This is where you'll jump."

The dirt-covered oval was surrounded by bench seating, tiers and tiers stretching up almost to the roof. Mary's eyes travelled slowly around the space. "Why are there so many seats?"

"For the spectators, of course. They'll fill every seat. The show jumping is a very popular event."

"I never thought about people watching. There must be seats for hundreds of people."

"Oh, close to a thousand I should think. Come on, let's find Henry and your brother and get something to eat. I'm starving."

There was so much to see and do that Mary had no time to be nervous. They ate Chinese food they bought from a booth at the fair, then wandered among the displays of handicrafts, baking and sewing. They admired exotic chickens, sheep dressed in blankets specially made to keep their wool clean, sleek, plump cattle and well-scrubbed pigs. They threw darts on the midway and drove the bumper cars, hooting with glee as they careened into one another. Every time Mary remembered the rows and rows of seats encircling the jumping ring, there was something to distract her: a juggling clown, a ride on a miniature train, the panorama of the city stretching out to reach the sea below her as she rode the Ferris wheel with her brother.

"Isn't it beautiful? Look, we're nearly as high as the mountains. Tom, your eyes are closed!"

"Darn right they are. And they're going to stay closed until I've got my boots back on solid ground where they belong."

The midway lights flicked on as the sun slipped down into the ocean. Dorothy consulted her program. "The Ladies' Show Hack is about to start. Let's go watch. Oh, but first we must have ice cream."

Licking their ice cream cones, they squeezed into the crowded grandstand.

"It's a full crowd tonight," observed Henry.

The grandstand spectators shifted over to make room for Dorothy and Mary.

"Thank you, that's so kind," said Dorothy. "This young lady wants to get a good look at the ring. She's riding in it tomorrow night. In the Open Jumping."

Heads turned to stare at Mary. "That little girl? Riding over those big jumps?" said one man, bushy eyebrows arched in amazement. "Well, she wouldn't be if she were my daughter. It's too dangerous. A man's horse fell on him last year and broke his leg. A grown man, not a child. Much too dangerous."

There were a few murmurs of assent. Mary felt her face grow warm.

"Don't listen," Dorothy whispered in her ear. "He's not a rider. He doesn't really know."

Mary nodded. Hemmed in by all these people, she suddenly felt very small.

"Let me take that." Dorothy plucked the melting ice cream cone out of her hand and dropped it in a nearby garbage can. She pressed a paper napkin into Mary's hand. "Wipe your chin."

"Ladies and gentlemen! Welcome to the first class of tonight's horse show: the Ladies' Show Hack."

One by one, a dozen finely bred horses strode regally into the ring below. Their polished coats and hooves gleamed under the bright lighting. Tiny braids emphasized the elegant arch of their necks, and tails flowed in silken falls from their muscled rumps. The riders' hands on the reins were gloved; immaculate white breeches and shining black boots completed their outfits. Each and every horse and rider pair was a perfect example of poised beauty. Captivated, Mary watched as they walked, trotted and cantered around the ring. The judge called for collected canter, and in response to invisible cues from the riders, the horses shortened their strides until they were like rocking horses, floating so gently their riders barely moved.

How would the judge choose? she wondered. How could he single out any one pair as better than all the others?

The horses and riders lined up in the centre of the ring. Without exception, the horses stood quietly. The winners were announced. From sixth place up, riders guided their horses forward to accept their ribbon. A silver trophy was handed to the first-place winner, and the crowd clapped and cheered.

Mary closed her eyes and let the waves of applause roll over her. Tomorrow night, in those very seats, another crowd would be cheering for the winner of the evening's jumping competition. Perhaps, just maybe, it would be Colleen.

Her eyelids jerked open. Slapping her hands together, she whistled and clapped along with the crowd, showing her approval as loudly as she could.

Sometime in the middle of the night, Mary woke with a start. She lay still on a strange bed, her heart thumping, and listened to the unfamiliar whoosh of traffic in the distance. Where was she?

A gentle snore reminded her. She was on a camp cot in makeshift living quarters in the back of the stock truck. Dorothy Zelinski slept in the other cot.

Mary rolled over, pulling her sleeping bag up. She needed to get back to sleep; she couldn't be tired tomorrow. She had to be at her best—she couldn't make a mistake, not in front of all those people. Rows and rows of seats, reaching high to the ceiling of the Livestock Pavilion, filled with people, a thousand or more, all watching her and Colleen.

"What am I doing here?" she whispered. "They're right, I'm too young. I'll let Colleen down, and Henry and Dorothy and Tom and Dad..." She broke off at the touch of a hand on her shoulder. She was certain she could smell the faint scent of lily of the valley.

Everything will be fine. Just fine. Now...rest.

"Mama," whispered Mary. A sense of peace flowed through her. Deeply comforted, she slept.

11

Early the next morning, hours before the fair opened to the public, Mary and Henry exercised their horses in the oval ring along with the other horse show competitors.

"Steady now, easy," Henry soothed as Vega bumped sideways into Colleen, startled by a Tennessee Walker flying past them at a running walk. The bay mare's eyes bulged and her neck was darkening with sweat. Like an angry cat's, her black tail lashed back and forth.

In contrast, Colleen was thriving on the horse show atmosphere. She was alert, her thin ears flicking as she took in all the new sights and sounds with great interest. Her confidence restored Mary's. They were a team, she and Colleen, and together they could do anything.

After exercise they returned the horses to their stalls and fed and watered them. Mary and Dorothy cleaned all the tack while Tom and Henry went to watch the beef cattle being judged.

The rest of the day passed quickly, and suddenly it was early evening. Mary changed into her riding clothes in the makeshift room in the back of the stock truck. She moved slowly, fumbling at buttons and zippers with shaking fingers. The hot dog Dorothy had urged her to eat threatened to come right back up.

Dorothy stuck her head around the curtain. "Are you ready?"

Mary shook her head mutely.

"Come on, get a move on. Tom's got your mare tacked up and you've got to walk the course. Mary, what's wrong?"

Mary clutched at her stomach, retching. Hastily, Dorothy thrust an empty bucket at her.

"Here, rinse your mouth out." Dorothy passed her a glass of water and then a damp face cloth. "Feel better now?"

"A little bit."

"Okay, then, let's go."

"I can't. I'm sick. I can't ride."

"Nerves, that's what you've got. You'll feel better once you're on your horse."

"Dorothy, I can't do this. I just can't."

"How do you know you can't? Mary, you haven't even tried."

"I just know. Not with all those people watching."

Dorothy sighed. "Well, I guess if you can't, you can't. But it's a long way to come for nothing."

"I know," said Mary miserably. "I'm sorry."

"Poor Colleen. She's in great form, just raring to go. You can tell she can't wait to get at those jumps. Tell you what, since you can't ride her, how about letting Henry?"

"No!"

"Why not?"

"Because...well, he's never ridden her before."

"That's no problem, not for Henry. He has such a way with horses. She's such a beautiful jumper. The crowd would love to see her. And she wants to jump. It seems such a pity to keep her from doing what she loves just because you're not well, especially when there's another rider available."

Mary drained the glass of water. "I'm starting to feel better. Maybe I just needed a drink of water."

"That's wonderful. Well, then, let's get over to the stables. Your steed awaits you." Dorothy parted the blanket with a flourish.

Mary crammed her hard hat onto her head and hopped down from the truck. The heels of her tall boots rang out on the pavement as she marched across the parking lot toward the Pavilion and her fate.

"After this fence there's a sharp turn and then three in a row. Make sure you line them up coming out of the corner. Mary, pay attention!" snapped Henry Zelinski.

Distracted by a large family squeezing into their ringside seats, Mary had missed Henry's instructions. She yanked her attention back to the task at hand. They were walking the jump course, following the numbered pattern through the brightly painted obstacles. Around them, other competitors were doing the same. Mary had noticed that, except for two women, both much older than she was, all the other riders were stern-faced men. They marched around the course without hesitation, obviously certain of their strategy and ability to remember the layout of the jumps.

"Hop, hop, hop, then turn this way and up and over the triple bar."

Mary stumbled after Mr. Zee in her stiff boots. She skidded to a halt in front of the triple bar. "But it's huge!"

Mr. Zee shrugged. "It's no problem for your horse. Come on!" Quickly he led her through the rest of the jumps. "That's it. Good course, eh?" He bounced on the toes of his boots, eager to get onto his horse.

Mary nodded weakly. The stands hummed with noise and activity, like a giant buzzing beehive.

They returned to their horses in the collecting ring. Still holding Colleen's reins, Tom boosted Mary into the saddle with one hand. He looked up into his sister's pale face. "How does the course look?"

Mary swallowed hard. "Tough. All those people in the stands! I've never seen so many. What if..."

"Go on," urged Tom. "Say it."

"What if I mess up? Everyone will be watching. They'll all see."

"You won't. Colleen won't. Mary, this is what you're good at. This is what you do."

Mary picked up the mare's reins. "Thanks, Tom. Now I've got to go practise a few jumps."

"I'll come along, Mary. I'll be right there if you need me."

Mary sat on Colleen just outside the gate into the ring. The mare's head was up as she watched the horse and rider inside, following their progress around the course. Mary leaned forward.

"You watch closely now, okay? We're going to be jumping in there next."

One ear flicked back to listen, but Colleen didn't take her eyes off the pair in the ring. They charged headlong down to the final fence, an enormous oxer, the rider tugging on the reins to slow his mount. The horse flung his head, fighting against the rider's stranglehold, his attention distracted until the jump was right there in front of him. Startled, the horse abruptly sat down, sliding into the jump and sending striped poles flying everywhere. The crowd gasped as the rider was flung into a jumble of toppled poles.

The judge blew his whistle and the ring crew rushed into action. Stiffly, the rider pushed himself to his feet, shaking off help. He hobbled over to catch his horse, who was nibbling at potted shrubs decorating the third jump, and pulled himself into the saddle.

In no time at all, the jump was back up. The whistle blew. The rider put his horse into a canter and aimed again for the jump. He dug his heels into the animal's sides. Head high, at least a stride too soon, the horse burst into the air as if he'd been shot out from a cannon.

Coming down, his hind legs hit the second rail of the jump. The red-and-white pole hit the dirt with a clunk that reverberated through the building.

Shaking his head grimly, the rider pulled up and turned his horse to the gate.

Mary realized the gate had swung open. "Come on now, young lady, in you go," said the whipper-in. "It's your turn."

Dimly, she was aware of voices behind her, offering her luck and good wishes, but they seemed to be coming from a long way away. Somehow Colleen was in the ring, trotting around the outside track, while the ring crew replaced the pole that had been knocked down. The mare held her head and neck high, her silver mane nearly touching Mary's chin. Her rib cage rose and fell as she took in great drafts of air, breathing the unfamiliar scents of a large number of human bodies sitting close together. Her gait was stiff and jerky, her ears swivelling back and forth, taking in all the unfamiliar noises.

There were so many sounds coming out of the stands as they rode by. Rustlings and cracklings and mutterings. A cackle of laughter, a hiss of rebuke. Chopped-up snippets of conversation—"...pretty gold colour... real high-stepper...she's a spirited one, for sure," as Colleen spooked at a child's balloon and wheeled away.

There was a hush as Mary got the horse under control. A voice rang out: "She's only a child! Look, John, she's a little girl."

Then the judge blew the whistle for Mary to begin her round.

For the longest moment of her life, Mary couldn't think what to do. Colleen was jigging underneath her, taut with nervous energy. Mary shifted in the saddle and the mare jumped into canter.

Left lead, that was good. The first fence was on the other side of the ring. Faces flew past in a blur as Colleen raced around the arena. "Easy now, steady, girl," Mary cajoled. She spotted the first obstacle with relief and steered toward it. She squeezed with her legs, even though they were already going too fast, not taking any chances of a refusal. There was a gasp of surprise and then cheers from the crowd as the palomino hurdled the fence like a steeplechaser.

They were back on the ground and moving, too fast for Mary to do anything but set her sights on the second fence. There was no time to think, no time to be nervous: the jump was four, three, two strides away. As Colleen put in one short stride before launching over the jump, Mary was looking ahead to the turn to the third.

A hind foot slipped out from under the mare in the loose dirt. Mary grabbed for the mane as Colleen caught her balance. She took off early, boldly launching over a big coop with a pair of solid-coloured rails on top. They landed far out, much too close to the next jump. Before Mary could even touch the reins, Colleen checked her stride, compressing her body and practically stretching up on tiptoes to fit in the stride. Over the vertical, then two short strides and they were up and over the oxer, clearing the fence by a foot, at least.

They were nearly at the end of the ring, galloping straight toward the stands. Hastily, Mary turned Colleen to the triple bar. The mare surged ahead. Mary recognized they were going too fast. The triple bar was wider than any other jump on the course. They had to leave the ground right in front of it to get over the width.

She tensed the reins and let go again right away, terrified of getting it wrong. Too close and Colleen wouldn't be able to stretch over the jump. But if they left too far out, the trajectory of her jump would bring them crashing down on the back rails.

Five feet from a good takeoff, Colleen took flight, leaping high into the air. Horrified, Mary ducked her head. She stared at the rails as they passed underneath the mare's belly—one, two, now three. Some corner of her mind realized the rails were far below them, farther than any jump had ever been before. Then they were descending, coming down on the far side of the jump. Coming down clear.

The force of landing tossed her up onto the mare's neck. She lost a stirrup. Colleen galloped around the ring while Mary struggled to get her boot back into the stirrup.

Without her pilot to guide her, the mare overshot

the next turn. Mary hauled her back on track to the brick wall. They were coming at an angle, but there was no time to alter their path. Mary traced a line through the centre of the jump. She sat very tall, eyes fixed on the far side of the wall, trusting her horse to choose the best spot to jump.

She did. Barely slowing her pace, Colleen reared up on her hindquarters and sprang over the wall. The spectators burst into cheers as the mare's head appeared above the huge obstacle, then her neck, her young rider's face buried in the mane, followed by her powerful golden body, tail flying out behind in a long stream of silver.

Two more jumps, easy efforts both, and they were done. Mary crouched over Colleen's withers as they raced through the finish line. The crowd's cheering swelled to a roar that echoed up into the domed ceiling. Colleen yanked the reins through Mary's fingers, bucking and tossing her head in her exuberance. Mary pitched in the saddle, both hands tangled in the mare's mane, gripping hard to hang on, and laughing with joy and relief. She caught glimpses of smiling faces, heard shouts of congratulation as they careened by the stands. Pulling her hands free, she took up the slack of the reins and eased Colleen to a walk, then halted in the middle of the ring.

Blowing hard, the mare raised her head high. Her gaze travelled along the stands. A fresh wave of applause rolled out and she bowed her head.

The next horse and rider came into the ring. "Our turn's over, Colleen," Mary said to her horse. Waving to the crowd, she rode her golden mare out of the ring.

Tom was at the gate. He reached up and pulled his sister down from the saddle.

"Did you see, Tom? Wasn't she wonderful?" Mary bounced on the toes of her boots.

Tom hugged her tight, lifting her off the ground. "You bet I saw. That was amazing!" He set her down. "I had no idea she could jump like that. Boy oh boy, Mary, how did you stay on? A couple of times I thought you were coming off for sure."

"Colleen would never let me fall. She wouldn't." Mary slid her stirrup irons up to the tops of the leathers and loosened the mare's girth. She couldn't resist— she flung her arms around her horse's damp neck. "Thank you, girl. Thank you so much."

"I'll walk her around so she cools off." Tom lifted the reins over Colleen's head.

Mary turned to see Henry beckoning her over. He walked Vega in circles around her. The bay mare's neck was dark with sweat. Her nostrils were flared as if she'd just finished jumping her round.

"Well done, Mary. I'm proud of you. Both of you." He gave her one of his rare smiles.

"Oh, Mary, that was wonderful!" Dorothy handed Mary a glass bottle. "Here, have a sip. It's ginger ale."

The soft drink tickled Mary's throat. She hiccupped softly. "It's good."

"Drink the rest if you want. You need to keep your energy up for the next round."

"The next round?"

"Yes, of course. So far three other riders have jumped clear. You will jump a second round against them, maybe a third or even a fourth until only one horse and rider have gone clear. Didn't Henry explain this to you?"

Mary nodded. "He did, but I wasn't thinking that far ahead."

"Henry Zelinski, you're in!" called the whipper-in.

12

"Good luck!" called Dorothy. "Come on, Mary, let's go watch from the stands."

The whistle had blown and Henry was cantering Vega to the first fence by the time they found seats. Distracted by the crowd, the bay mare was surprised to find a jump a few strides ahead. She veered off but Henry got her back on track. He pressed on and the mare jumped high headed, like a deer.

"Come on, Vega, pay attention," urged Dorothy. She crossed her fingers. Mary did the same.

"She's settling down now," said Mary. "She's jumping much better."

"She is, isn't she? That's jump four clear. Now five. Henry's going to do it, I know he is. He's going to get her around clear!"

Henry seemed to do barely anything in the saddle. His aids to his horse were so subtle that Vega appeared to be jumping completely on her own. Yet Mary knew he was somehow exerting tremendous influence over the high-strung mare. She covered the ground in steady, even strides before leaping over the jumps with inches to spare. At the triple bar, Vega snapped her knees nearly up to her outstretched head as she soared. A smattering of applause shattered her poise and sent her scooting through the corner. Gently, Henry brought her under control again. He turned her toward the wall.

The mare's strides were stiff and choppy. Somehow Henry sat her as if she were smooth as a rocking horse. The set of his chin and the unwavering focus of his eyes declared his determination to get over the jump in their path. Vega felt his resolution. Her ears snapped forward, her attention on the wall. She moved toward the jump with purpose.

Her hindquarters coiled. Her neck lifted, front legs began to fold at the knees.

Across the arena, Mary heard a child shrieking. Then she saw a bright red helium balloon rising slowly from the stands. A draft caught it up, dancing the balloon out of the stands and over the jumping course.

Rising up on her hind legs to push off, Vega caught sight of the red balloon. She plunged down, spinning around to avoid colliding with the wall. Henry was thrown over her shoulders, one arm flung out around the mare's neck. She ducked away, startled, but somehow Henry still had the reins and pulled her to a stop. In one smooth movement he was back in the saddle again, urging Vega into canter and turning her to face the wall.

"He's going to try again!" cried Mary.

"He is! He certainly is! Look, look, he did it! He got

her over!" Dorothy clasped her hands together under her chin. "He's going to finish!"

A brief cheer greeted Vega and Henry as they touched down after clearing the wall. Then a hush fell over the audience as he galloped on to the final jumps. Vega lifted over the second to last and charged on. "Steady now. Easy, girl." Henry's voice rang out clearly in the hushed silence. Closing in deep on the final fence, Vega reared up and sprang into the air. For a moment it seemed she'd misjudged, had jumped too low. Mary tensed, waiting for the clunk of a heavy wooden pole slamming onto the dirt.

Still airborne, Vega kicked out with her hind feet. The top pole rattled in its cups as her hooves skimmed over it. Then she was down and galloping away and the pole was still in place.

As loud as a hundred drums, clapping burst out of the stands. All around Dorothy and Mary, spectators were scrambling to their feet to cheer. Henry galloped a circuit, his hat in his hand to salute the crowd. Dorothy stood at the railing, waving. He held his hand over his heart and grinned up at her.

Clapping as hard as everyone around her, Mary shut her eyes to replay the magnificent display of horsemanship she'd just seen.

Dorothy tugged her to her feet. "You've got to get ready for the jump-off."

She pulled Mary along with her out of the stands down to the collecting ring. Henry was still smiling, patting and stroking Vega. He vaulted from the saddle and hugged his wife.

"That was marvellous, Henry! Just marvellous! You rode her so well. If only that balloon hadn't spooked her, she might have jumped clear."

Henry shrugged. "These things happen. She tried very hard, didn't you, my Vega?"

"If only she were like Valiant," sighed Dorothy. "He loves competing. The bigger the crowd, the higher he jumps." She lifted the reins over the mare's head and led her away.

Henry pointed at the wall where a drawing of the second-round jump course was posted. "Just six jumps this round. Of course, they'll be raised."

Mary traced the route with her finger.

The last rider in round one came out of the gate, shaking his head. "Twelve faults," he grumbled. The ring crew hurried in to raise the jumps.

Tom returned with Colleen. The mare's girth was tightened, the stirrup irons were pulled down and Mary was tossed up into the saddle.

"Are you ready?" asked Henry. The first rider in the jump-off was in the ring waiting for the whistle.

Colleen stood outside the gate, her ears pricked. The whistle blew and she snatched at the bit, eager for her turn.

"We are," Mary replied. "We're ready."

The rider on course was halfway around, reining his horse in hard between jumps to go very slowly, and then rushing the last few strides to make a spectacular leap over the obstacle. Riding hard to the triple, they left the ground too close to the jump. The horse's hind legs trailed over the highest rail and toppled it to the ground.

"That's the second rail down," said Henry. "And now a third."

The gate opened.

"It's your turn now. Good luck, Mary. Remember to trust your horse."

Mary rode Colleen in. The first rider passed her on his way out, his horse sweating and jigging. "Good luck, miss. Be careful, it's a tough course. Especially for a young lady."

She barely heard him. She was aware of the now familiar murmuring and rustling of the audience, the glare of the lights overhead, the tang of the dirt rising up from the floor. Beneath her, Colleen was alert, moving with energy but waiting for Mary's signal. The mare understood her part. So did her rider. Now, more than ever, they were a team.

The whistle shrilled. The crowd became quiet. Mary touched Colleen and they were cantering, skipping toward the first jump.

It loomed before them, higher than anything they'd jumped before. Resolutely, Mary set her gaze above it, treating it as if it were just any old fence on the ranch and not the biggest obstacle they'd ever tackled in front of more people than she'd ever seen in her entire life.

She tightened her legs against her horse's sides and chirped. The slender golden ears were almost at Mary's chin. The mare's head came higher, her front legs folding and lifting. She crouched down on her hind legs and pushed off, soaring over the jump. Mary reached forward until her arms were completely straight, giving the mare total freedom from the bit. She was folded tight against the horse's neck and withers, her face brushing against the silver mane. They seemed to be hanging in the air above the jump; then Colleen's neck was dipping away beneath and they were coming down, landing with a force that surprised Mary. She flopped onto the mare's neck, reins flapping loose. She pushed herself upright but there was no time to shorten the reins. Colleen was galloping, heading in a direction that took her away from the second jump.

Mary pulled hard to turn her back. The mare swung around. Elbows pumping, Mary urged her at the jump. Colleen shot forward and launched into the air, stretching her body to clear the width of the double rails. Mary heard laughter and realized it was her own.

She looked ahead to the next fence, ready to guide her horse the moment her hooves returned to earth. Gallop, jump, land, turn; gallop, jump, land, turn— in perfect rhythm they danced around the course, the crowd cheering them on.

They bounded over the last fence. A great roar rolled out of the stands. Mary gave Colleen her head, galloping around the outside of the arena close to the fans. As sure-footed as a cat, the golden mare raced at breakneck speed, her silver tail streaming out behind her.

The next competitor was in the ring, glaring at them as he trotted his horse in circles, waiting for them to leave. Giving and taking on the reins, Mary managed to slow Colleen to a prancing walk. She swiped the back of her wrist over her eyes, wiping away tears of joy.

The crowd was still clapping as they exited the ring. Congratulations came at her from all sides, but Mary barely heard them. Her heart was still thudding against her ribs. She'd never felt so happy, so delighted, so...so humble. She slid from her saddle and threw her arms around Colleen's neck. The lump in her throat kept her from speaking, but her horse, her partner, felt her thanks. For a few moments Colleen held still, her restless spirit quiet.

Then, with a deep sigh, she shook all over and began to fidget and fuss. Tom took her from Mary. "I'll walk her for you."

"Don't go far," said Henry. "There may be another jump-off."

There wasn't. Not another horse and rider made it over the course clear.

"Well, that's that," said Henry, rubbing his hands together as the last rider slunk through the gate in defeat. "Come on now, Mary, up you get. Don't keep them waiting. And congratulations. You did well, very well."

The grandstand erupted in a storm of cheering and clapping as Mary and Colleen led a parade of horses and riders back into the ring. They lined up before a table that had been quickly brought out. Bright ribbons covered the tabletop, and in the centre was a large trophy sporting a silver model of a jumping horse and rider. In a dreamlike daze, Mary smiled and clapped politely as a well-fed gentleman, important in a suit, straw hat and polished shoes, came forward. He pinned a ribbon to each horse's bridle and shook the rider's hand. He started at the far end of the line, and when he reached Mary he picked up the silver trophy and carried it over.

"Well done, young lady! Very impressive performance! Your mare is a marvel. Made it look easy, she did. Wonderful horse, natural jumper!"

He patted Colleen's neck heartily before passing the trophy up to Mary. It was surprisingly heavy.

"Over here, miss," called a photographer. "Big smile!" Mary blinked at the glare of the flash from the camera.

The photographer let the camera hang from a strap around his neck and pulled a notepad and a pencil from his pocket. He scribbled down Mary's and Colleen's names and where they were from. When he was done writing he reached up and shook Mary's hand. "Miss Inglis, I admire your bravery in riding such a spirited animal over such high jumps. It was something to watch."

The other riders had gone back to the stalls. The trophy table had been taken away, and the ring crew was dismantling the jumps. Mary turned Colleen around and rode out of the arena.

At the exit she stopped Colleen and looked back, reliving those wonderful, triumphant moments of leaping high, slipping free of gravity's hold to soar through the air, and knew nothing would ever be the same again.

She'd tasted glory and it had left her hungry for more.

13

"It's not quite champagne, but it will have to do!" Dorothy handed Mary a mug of ginger ale.

Henry rose to his feet. "Up, up, everyone, please!" He held his mug aloft. "I'd like to propose a toast."

"Hear, hear!" said Dorothy.

"To Mary and her Colleen. May this win be the first of many. I am certain it will!"

"To Mary and Colleen," echoed Tom and Dorothy, holding their mugs high.

"Thank you," said Mary. The three faces smiling at her began to blur and she realized she had tears in her eyes.

A man's head appeared through the curtain of the tack room. "Henry Zelinski? Is that really you?"

"Charlie Peters! What are you doing here? Come in, come in!"

"Oh my goodness, Charlie, I can't believe it's you!" said Dorothy.

A round-faced man in a well-cut suit that didn't quite hide his paunch squeezed into the stall. He removed his hat and hugged Dorothy. "It is, Dorothy. I'm glad to see you're as beautiful as ever. And Henry! Managed to get away from the ranch, did you?"

"Just for a few days. Listen, Charlie, I have to thank you again for recommending me for the position."

Charlie Peters waved away Henry's thanks. "You're the best man for the job. And all I did was write a letter. So you like it there, eh?"

"Very much."

"Getting along with Simon Dalton?"

Henry shot a quick glance at Tom and Mary. "He hasn't been around much. Not at all, actually."

"He's a busy man."

"Yes, I know. Charlie, let me introduce you to Mary Inglis and her brother, Tom. Charlie's an old friend. We used to ride in horse shows against each other."

"And you still do, I see. It's too bad about that bay you're on. She's not the most reliable animal, hmm? But the palomino, now there's a jumper for you."

"That's Mary's own horse, Colleen. She's something, isn't she?" said Dorothy.

Charlie Peters swung around to face Mary. "So you're the owner of that wonderful mare?"

She nodded.

"Well, aren't you a lucky girl. Where did you find her?"

"My dad got her for me."

"Did he? But from where?"

"The range."

Charlie Peters narrowed his brown eyes. "You're telling me that horse is a cayuse?" He snorted in disbelief.

"She was born wild, sir," said Tom firmly. "Our father got her young and raised her up for Mary here."

"Why all the interest, Charlie?" asked Henry. "Are you thinking about taking up jumping again? You'll have to get fit if you are."

"No, no, I'm not getting back in the saddle. But I am getting back into the sport. I have just been appointed chef d'équipe of our country's show jumping team."

"Charlie! Congratulations!" said Dorothy. "You're exactly the right man for the job. With you in charge, the team will be better than ever."

"Thank you. I'll do my best. Anyway, that's why I'm here tonight. I'm scouting out horses and riders for the team. The next Olympic Games are only a year away and we need to be well prepared. I'm determined this team will win a medal. Preferably the gold medal. To do that we'll need a strong team. Experienced riders and athletic horses."

"You've got your work cut out for you, my friend," said Henry.

"I know." He turned back to Mary. "So tell me, Miss Inglis, would you like to see that superb mare of yours representing your country?"

"You mean in the Olympics? Oh, yes!"

"Good, good, glad to hear it. And how about you, Henry? Ready to ride on the national team again?"

"Of course! But I have to let you know, Charlie, that I'm under-horsed. Valiant isn't up to the job anymore, and Vega, well, she just doesn't have the heart. I'm afraid that I've got nothing else."

"Oh dear, I'm afraid I haven't made myself clear. I was proposing for you to ride Mary's palomino. What do you say?" He beamed at Mary.

"Colleen's not for sale," said Mary.

"Mary's a good rider. Why can't she *and* her horse be on the team together?" asked Tom.

Charlie settled onto a tack trunk. "How old is your sister?"

"Nearly fifteen, sir. Her birthday's in less than two months."

"Well, there's one answer: Mary's too young. You have to be eighteen to be on the Olympic team. But that's not the only problem. You see, although women are now allowed to compete in the equestrian events in the Games, they are not permitted to jump."

"What?" Tom raked his hand through his hair. "Why not?"

Charlie shrugged. "Because the powers that be decided in 1951 that jumping at that level is too dangerous for women. The jumps are too big and the courses too long—women don't have the strength or stamina to get around."

"Oh, Charlie, that's such hogwash!" said Dorothy.

"Hey, don't blame me! I don't make the rules."

Tom slung his arm around his sister's shoulders. "Those are pretty much the stupidest rules I've ever heard of. They need to be changed."

"But they are the rules. I can't have a woman on my jumping team. I'm sorry, Mary, but that's just the way it is."

Mary shrugged, too disappointed to speak.

"So here's the situation: an experienced rider with no horse and a dynamite horse just begging to jump. How about it, Mary? You don't have to sell your mare. Just *lend* her to the team, to Henry. Not forever. Just for the Olympics."

"No! No, I won't do it! She's mine."

"And she still would be. Think of it, Mary, you'd be the owner of an Olympic horse. That would be something to be proud of. Perhaps I should talk to your father. After all, this is a decision for an adult to make. Is he here?"

"He's not," said Tom. "You can ask him, Mr. Peters, and he'll tell you the same thing: the horse is Mary's."

"Just the same, I'd like to talk to him directly. What is his telephone number?"

"We don't have a telephone."

"All right, your address then. I'll write a letter."

"Charlie, no," said Henry. "The horse belongs to the girl, belongs *with* Mary. It's too much to ask."

"If you say so." Charlie sighed. "Well, I'll just have to find another mount for you, Henry, somehow, somewhere. Unless, of course, there are more cayuses that jump like deer roaming the range on that ranch of Dalton's?"

"No, sir, not a one," said Tom. "The rest are just ordinary wild horses."

"So the mare's one of a kind. What a pity." He shook his head sadly. "Well, Mary, if you ever change your mind..."

"I won't, Mr. Peters. I won't ever change my mind."

"I see. Well, that's that, I suppose." Charlie Peters crossed his arms in front of his chest and sighed heavily.

An awkward silence fell.

"It's so wonderful to see you again, Charlie," said Dorothy brightly. "Remember that time in Toronto, at the Royal Winter Fair, when you and Henry dressed up as Tweedledum and Tweedledee for the pairs jumping? That was such fun! Even the judges were laughing. Remember, they forgot to score that knockdown and declared you the winners?"

"How could I forget? And what about the time in Winnipeg when I went off course and jumped half the course backward?"

"The judge whistled so hard trying to stop you that he ran out of air!" recalled Henry. "And you just kept on jumping."

"I was concentrating so hard I didn't hear a thing! Too bad, I jumped a clear round. That was on Nobleman, remember him?"

"I sure do. I rode him too, for Mrs. McArthur."

"That's right, when I had a broken collarbone. Man, that horse could jump! Pulled like a freight train, but he'd go over anything you pointed him at. Wonderful horse, just wonderful."

Leaning on her brother's shoulder, Mary listened with fascination to the tales of past triumphs and struggles. A few months ago she had known this world existed but couldn't imagine ever being part of it. Now that she was, how could she not aspire to be the very best, to compete at the pinnacle of the sport? The ache in her heart made her restless. She got to her feet.

"I'm going to check on the horses," she announced. The chatter continued behind her as she slipped out of the tack room.

Vega stood at the front of her stall, ears flicking as she listened to the sounds of the fair outside the stables. Mary checked her hay and water and straightened her stable sheet. She stroked the soft neck the colour of dark chocolate. In her own way Vega had given her best. Henry was right; the dark bay mare just didn't have the heart for competition jumping.

Colleen was lying down in the next stall. She looked up as Mary entered but didn't move to get to her feet. Mary sat down in the straw, settling into the curve of the mare's neck. She rested her face on the long ridged crest, feeling the silky tickle of the mane on her cheek.

"You like being here, don't you, girl?" she whispered. "Just like me. It's not what we're used to, but somehow it's where we belong."

She closed her eyes to relive their evening of triumph once again. Beside her, Colleen sighed, her nostrils fluttering, and Mary knew her best friend and partner was remembering their soaring, glorious performance too.

"Tonight was only the beginning, Colleen," she whispered. "This was just the start."

14

"There, Colleen, there we are." Mary held open the scrapbook. A single newspaper clipping filled the entire first page. She pointed to a black-and-white photograph of Colleen with her head high, gazing into the distance while Mary grinned at the camera. "Don't you look beautiful?"

The mare lifted her head from her grazing to sniff at the scrapbook. Sitting cross-legged on the grass, Mary reached out and smoothed her horse's pale silver forelock. Colleen pulled her head away and shook the hair into a muss again. She went back to eating.

"Here, let me read you what it says.

"*Girl wonder triumphs in jumping debut at horse show.*

"*A young amazon mounted on a golden steed took the top place in the feature jumping competition at the Pacific National Exhibition. Flying over obstacles as high as her horse's head, fourteen-year-old Mary Inglis won out over competitors twice her age and more. Adding to the glory of Miss Inglis's accomplishment was the fact that this was the first jumping competition she and her mount had ever entered. With modesty becoming a young lady,*

Mary Inglis gives full credit to her horse, Colleen. 'She did it all. I just told her which way to go and stayed on.'"

Mary broke off reading, captivated by the memory of that wonderful day. She lay back in the cool, irrigated grass of Colleen's pasture, the scrapbook clasped tight. Soothed by the steady munching of the mare's strong teeth and the rising dusk chorus of cicadas, she closed her eyes to re-experience each detail, even the churning of her stomach that, looking back, was just a bit of discomfort, quickly overshadowed by the joy of flying over those enormous jumps.

"Colleen? Do you dream about it too? When you're standing here in the shade under the trees with your eyes closed, are you remembering what it felt like?"

The mare heaved a long sigh.

"I thought so," Mary whispered.

"There you are."

Mary's eyes opened to see her father leaning on the pasture fence, his boot propped on the bottom rail.

"What do you have there?" He pointed his chin at the scrapbook.

She scrambled to her feet. "Look, Dorothy got it for me. She said I'm going to need something to keep all the newspaper clippings and photographs in. Wasn't it nice of her?"

"Real nice," Dad agreed. He took the scrapbook and studied the lone newspaper clipping as if it were the first time he'd seen it, though Mary knew he'd read it many times since they'd brought it home with them from Vancouver two weeks ago. "Mrs. Zee's a nice lady. The mister's okay too. Once you get used to his ways, he's a decent man."

"We're lucky they came here to the ranch, aren't we, Dad?"

"We are. Speaking of coming here to the ranch, the Daltons arrived this afternoon with a couple of guests."

Mary glanced back at her horse, still grazing peacefully under the trees. "I'll move her to the back pasture right away."

Dad shook his head. "Hold up a moment. Seems that Mrs. Zee's been bragging you up. She sent that same newspaper clipping you've got in your book to the Daltons."

"Oh, no!" Mary's heart began to pound. "Why did she do that?"

"She's proud of you, Mary. She meant well. The thing is, well, now the Daltons want to see you...and Colleen."

"No! They can't! You know that."

"I don't see how we can stop them."

"We can hide her. Move her to another field, put her in a shed. I know! I'll take her up into the mountains and camp out until they're gone. You can send Tom to let me know."

"Mary, listen! They want to see you jumping Colleen. Mr. Zee asked if you could go to the jumping field tomorrow morning and ride her over a few fences for the Daltons and their guests. He said they're eager to see the girl wonder and her golden steed perform."

"This is all my fault. I should never have gone in that horse show," groaned Mary. "It was showing off, just like you said. I should have stayed here on the ranch with Colleen."

"Mary, you did the right thing. An opportunity came along and you grabbed hold of it." Dad squinted into the glare of the setting sun. "They say hindsight's twenty-twenty and that sure is the truth. I should have spoken up and told Mr. Dalton years ago about your horse. I should have gotten things settled when she was still a greenbroke filly."

"Why didn't you, Dad?"

"Well, back then I thought she was just going to be a nice riding horse for my daughter. I didn't think it was worth stirring up any fuss over her. Never crossed my mind the two of you would go on and do what you've done."

"But what about tomorrow, Dad? What do I do?"

"Well, maybe we've been giving Simon Dalton too much credit."

"What do you mean?"

"He comes here once, maybe twice, a year. Hardly knows his way around the place. In fact, it's probably just luck if he remembers his way to the kitchen in the big house for his dinner."

"He eats in the dining room, remember?"

"Oh, right. The point is, Mr. Dalton most likely

doesn't remember as much about what happens on this ranch as we think he does. I'd say the chances of him putting two and two together when he sees your mare are pretty small."

"I don't want to take any chances, Dad. Not with Colleen. I want to keep her hidden and not lose her."

"So, no more jumping. No more horse shows. You've been over the moon since you came back from the coast. You'd give that up?"

Mary hesitated, just for a moment, before nodding. "I would."

"What about the Zees? What are you going to tell them?"

"I'll say I don't want to jump anymore. I'll say I don't like it. That I'm scared of falling off and getting hurt."

Dad pulled off his hat and turned it over. "You'd be lying."

"I know."

"Don't do it, Mary. Don't lie. Go over there tomorrow and jump your mare. This is something the two of you are good at—darned good—and it would be a crime to hide that away, all because you're afraid of something that probably will never happen. So go and show them. Hold your head high and show them how it's done."

"Dad, I can't!" Mary wailed. She clasped the scrapbook tight to her chest. "I just can't!"

She stumbled forward onto her knees as someone pushed her from behind. "Hey!" She flung out her hands to catch her balance, and the scrapbook tumbled to the grass. "Colleen, what did you do that for?"

Mary crouched on her haunches, reaching for the scrapbook. It had fallen open to the single newspaper clipping. Colleen sniffed at the page, her nostrils fluttering. Her ears came forward to attention as her dark eyes seemed to study the photo and article. Seconds went by. Then she let out a long sigh.

"Well, I never," said Dad softly.

Colleen raised her head and looked at Mary, still hunkered down. The mare reached over and bunted her again with her muzzle before returning her gaze to the scrapbook.

A shiver ran down Mary's spine. Colleen was trying to tell her something, and she was certain she knew what it was. She got to her feet. "All right, then. We'll do it. We'll jump." She threw her arms around the mare's neck. "I won't keep you from doing what you love, just to keep you safe with me."

Dad cleared his throat a few times. "Must have swallowed too much dust today."

"Dad, I'm going to make you proud of me."

"Miss Mary, you do that every day," her father said gruffly.

15

As Mary rode to the jumping field the next morning, her resolve weakened. More than once she was tempted to rein Colleen around, ready to head up into the mountains to hide away until the Daltons were long gone from the ranch.

When Colleen realized where they were going, there was no turning back. The mare arched her golden neck as she pranced along the road into the ranch yard, then past the barn to the jumping field beyond. Her head came up high to take in the small crowd gathered beside a long table that was covered with a white cloth and laden with serving dishes.

Mary caught sight of rows of chairs set out by the jumps. Her mouth went dry. She'd been expecting Dorothy and Henry and the Daltons, maybe a guest or two. Not all these people.

As she rode closer, she spotted Joe Pettit and his wife, Patricia, chatting with some of the ranch hands. Relieved to recognize people she knew, she looked around for other familiar faces.

"There you are!" Dorothy turned away from a small

group and hurried up to Mary. "The star attraction has arrived! Mary, what is it?"

"What's he doing here?" Mary jerked her chin at the people Dorothy had just left.

"Who, Mary?" Dorothy turned to look back.

"That Mr. Peters. From Vancouver. Why is he here?"

"He's a guest of the Daltons. He's come for a visit with them." Dorothy lifted her eyebrows. "You are going to be polite to my guests, aren't you? Because just now, the tone of your voice was quite rude, you know."

"I'm sorry." Mary pressed her teeth into her lip, bitterly regretting that she hadn't acted on her first instinct, to flee with Colleen.

"Come and meet everyone. But first, put on that pretty smile of yours. That's better."

Dorothy took Colleen's bridle and led her and Mary to where Henry was listening attentively to a man with a very broad girth in a western suit. Beside him, a woman with dark, curled hair, wearing a full-skirted gingham dress, fanned herself with one hand and laughed at a remark from Charlie Peters.

"Diana, Simon, Charlie, may I present Miss Mary Inglis." Dorothy let go of Colleen and stepped back beside her husband.

"Well, Mary, I wouldn't have recognized you," boomed Simon Dalton. "Look at you, all grown up." He barely glanced at Colleen.

"Hello, Mary." Diana Dalton smiled kindly up at her. "You may not remember us. We don't get out here to the ranch as often as we'd like."

Mr. Dalton pulled Henry aside. His whisper was loud enough for everyone to overhear. "The horse wrangler's girl, is she? What's his name again? Oh, right, Donny Inglis. Now I remember."

Mary smiled shyly at Mrs. Dalton. "I do remember you a little bit, ma'am."

"It's wonderful to hear that you're doing so well with your riding. Henry Zelinski thinks very highly of you and your beautiful horse."

"Thank you. Mr. Zee has helped me so much. So has Mrs. Zee."

"Mr. and Mrs. Zee? Is that what you call them? Well, Zelinski is a mouthful, no doubt about it," said Diana Dalton.

Mary sighed, her tension easing. Not a single question about Colleen. Her mouth curved into a genuine smile as her heart lightened with relief.

Not only had she grown up in the past seven years, but the Daltons had gotten older. Laugh lines crinkled the corners of Diana's eyes, and the hair at Simon Dalton's temples was distinctly grey.

"Hello, Mary! Pleasure to see you again!" said Charlie Peters. He patted Colleen's neck. "And your marvellous mare."

Dorothy was too busy chatting to notice, so Mary ignored him.

Henry beckoned to Mary. "Come with me." He took her over to the jumps and outlined the course. "When you're done, ride over to the seating area. Mr. Dalton wants to give a little speech. He's very proud, you know."

"Why? He barely remembers me."

"Because you're from the ranch. His ranch. Your success reflects back onto him. Do you understand?"

"Not really."

"We'll get going as soon as everyone is sitting down. Warm up Colleen while you're waiting. I'll give you the signal to begin."

Mary trotted and cantered Colleen while Dorothy and Henry herded the guests onto seats. At Henry's wave, Mary turned her horse to the first fence.

"Here we go, girl," she whispered.

Locking in on the obstacle in her path, Colleen surged forward, eager to conquer it. She rocketed over the oxer, leaping up so high that Mary felt herself begin to tip back. Hastily, she grabbed the mare's mane. There was a gasp from the small crowd and then wild cheering as the golden mare and her rider cleared the double rails with at least a foot to spare.

Mary felt her braids hit her shoulders as they returned to earth. She tried to gather up the reins, but Colleen shook them free again and charged on. Mary realized she was on a different horse. Headstrong with confidence, the mare wanted to jump her own way. All her rider could do was direct her at the fences.

They galloped at the barrels. Up and over and away. Now the turn across the middle. Mary tightened the reins and felt Colleen resist. Tactfully, carefully, she pulsed the pressure until the mare yielded and turned. A wall of blue-and-white rails stood in front of them. Launching off the ground well back from the jump, Colleen arched her body to clear the height. Just a few strides and they were tackling the triple combination: jump, one stride, jump, two strides, jump. Mary laughed out loud with joy as they landed clear.

Colleen's ear flicked back, wanting direction. Mary focused on the green coop set right in the middle of the short side of the course. From between the twin golden ears she saw the wide ramp coming closer and closer. Colleen kicked out in scorn as they sailed over.

Another turn, Colleen tossing her head against the bit. Rails over the ditch, then the wall. Mary struggled to get the mare around the last two corners, until she sighted the triple bar in the middle of the course and raced at it. Her neck reared up, knocking Mary hard on the chin—the mare was taking off at least a stride too soon. Mary stared down at the three ascending poles for endless moments as they hovered above them, Colleen dropping down to land at last with a force that nearly tossed her rider over her shoulder.

Mary scrambled back in the saddle, but it was too late. Colleen had run right past the last fence. She yanked hard on one rein, pulling the mare down to a jigging trot before she got her turned around. "Come on, girl, there's another jump."

She could not get the mare to go in a straight line. Finally, after zigzagging around the other jumps, she had her back on track to the final obstacle. Colleen was still trotting, but Mary was determined to finish the course. At this pace the jump seemed enormous. Resolutely, Mary fixed her eyes above the top rail. She chirped and Colleen stood up on her hind legs like a circus horse. She sprang into the air and over the jump.

"Whoa now, girl, whoa." Mary turned Colleen in smaller and smaller circles until the mare consented to walk. Her neck had dampened to bronze and she was blowing hard, but she was still prancing as they moved away from the jumps. The chairs were abandoned. All the guests were on their feet, clapping and whistling. Puffing for air, Mary waved, and a fresh burst of cheering broke out.

Mr. Dalton gave a short speech of congratulation before coming over and shaking Mary's hand.

"Range bred, you say," Charlie Peters said to Dad.

Mary looked over and saw her father nodding.

"I still say there must be some Thoroughbred blood in her." Dorothy's clear voice rose above the chatter.

Simon Dalton turned back to look at Colleen. His eyes narrowed.

Mary stared at Dorothy. *Be quiet,* she implored silently. *Please, don't say anything more.*

"Simon," Dorothy called, "was there ever anyone around here with a Thoroughbred stallion? Perhaps even a Thoroughbred mare."

Stricken, Mary searched for her father, but her eyes met Charlie Peters' instead.

"Yes," said Mr. Dalton. "Yes, someone did have a Thoroughbred mare. A very well-bred mare, brought up all the way from Kentucky."

"Aha! I knew it! Who was it, Simon? Who did she belong to?"

Simon Dalton didn't reply. He turned his head, searching through his employees. When he got to Dad, his mouth tightened in an expression of absolute fury.

16

"Where did you get her, Donny?" Simon Dalton demanded.

Dad crossed his arms. He looked past Mr. Dalton into the distance. "My girl's horse is my business."

His voice was calm and level. He stood with his feet slightly apart. Mary recognized his stance. She'd seen him use it many times with unsettled green horses, standing quietly in the middle of the corral until they finished racing about and turned to the steadfast man beside them for guidance.

It wasn't working with Simon Dalton. "I know who the mare is, Donny. I recognize her now."

Dad didn't say anything.

Now Mr. Dalton crossed his arms. "Inglis, we will get to the bottom of this."

They stood in a corner of the jumping field, in the shade of a small grove of aspens. Mr. Dalton had led the way to this spot, declaring he wanted a word with Donny Inglis and his daughter. Mary slid down and led Colleen beside her father. Tom fell in beside them. Diana Dalton and the Zelinskis had stayed back, but

Mary saw them casting anxious glances their way as they directed the packing up of the buffet table and the chairs. Soon everything was loaded on a hay wagon to be taken back to the big house. The ranch hands moved off, shaking their heads. No one ever spoke of it, but everyone who'd been on the ranch for any amount of time was aware of who Colleen was. They also knew of the bond between the horse and her girl.

Now Mrs. Dalton was picking her way over the field in her high heels, clutching Charlie Peters' arm for support. Henry and Dorothy followed right behind.

"Simon, what is this all about?" asked his wife.

"Do you remember some years back when I brought in that mare from Kentucky?"

"That lovely chestnut with the blaze? Yes, of course I do. You trucked her all the way to Kelowna to breed her to George Finlay's Thoroughbred stallion. You and George were so very excited; you both were sure you had a winning racehorse on the way. But the foal—it was a filly, wasn't it?—died as a weanling. You were so discouraged you sold the mare."

"That's right, Diana, that's just about how it happened."

"Just about?"

"The truth is, the filly didn't die. Donny Inglis here took her."

Diana gasped. "Donny! You stole that filly?"

"I did not!" said Dad. "Mr. Dalton told me to get rid of her. Those were his exact words."

"So, you admit this mare is that filly?" said Simon Dalton.

"All I'm saying is what you told me to do."

"Oh, Simon, you didn't, did you?" asked Diana. "An innocent young animal. You didn't mean for Donny to..." She couldn't finish.

"No, no, of course not! Inglis misunderstood me. I was disappointed, as you said. I just wanted him to take her away, before anyone saw her."

"But why?" asked Diana. "Why wouldn't you want that filly after all the work you did to get her?"

"Because she wasn't—isn't—full Thoroughbred. George's horse is dark bay, nearly black. The mare was chestnut. The foal came out palomino."

"Was there another stallion at the breeding farm?" asked Charlie.

Simon shook his head. "Only the one."

"So what happened?"

Simon Dalton rubbed his hand over his face. "There's a palomino stallion with the wild horses. He must have come down right into the ranch yard. A cayuse stallion!" He laughed bitterly.

Diana patted his arm. "I am sorry. You were so excited about that foal. You boasted about it to everyone. Yes, dear, you *were* boasting."

"I felt like a fool when I saw that yellow filly. A complete idiot."

"But, Simon, you *have* bred a winner," said Charlie. "Not a racehorse but a winning jumper!"

"Hang on there," said Dad. "No one can say this is the same horse, not for sure."

"Oh, come on, look at her! You can see she's got good Thoroughbred blood in her, just like Dorothy says."

"But I didn't mean...I didn't know...Oh, I feel awful! I wish I hadn't said anything!" Dorothy covered her face with her hands.

Me too, thought Mary, glaring at Dorothy. *Why didn't you keep quiet?*

"Mary, I'm so sorry." Dorothy reached out and took Mary's hand.

Mary pulled away. She shut her eyes so she wouldn't have to see the woman's stricken face. Tears burned behind her eyelids. The worst fear of her life, the trap she'd always looked out for, had opened up in front of her and she hadn't even seen it lying there. Like an idiot she'd fallen in and taken Colleen with her.

"Inglis, tell me to my face this isn't the filly out of my good Thoroughbred mare," said Simon Dalton.

Dad looked over at Mary. His black eyes were filled with sorrow. Donny Inglis prided himself on being an honest man. "She is," he admitted. "But you told me to get rid of her. You didn't want her. So I brought her home to my daughter."

Mary remembered that wonderful morning. She and Tom had been playing circus with Mike on the scrubby patch of grass behind their little house when a whinny shook Mike's sturdy body. Another horse whinnied back, and there was Dad leading an elegant red mare down the ranch road, a leggy filly foal pressed up against her flank.

Mary cried out in delight. The filly was as pretty as an Easter chick, all soft yellow fuzz except for the white wool of her curly mane and little tail. She had a white blaze down the middle of her face and white socks on her two back legs.

"Dad, what are you doing with Mr. Dalton's mare and foal?" Tom asked.

Dad just said, "Give me a hand cleaning out the shed."

When the shed was ready, Dad brought the mare and her foal in. Then he turned the mare around, took her out and led her away, back down to the ranch yard where she couldn't see her filly or hear her frantic whinnies.

Listening to the weanling's squealing, Mary felt her heart squeezed to pulp. She peered through a crack and saw the filly dashing around the makeshift stall, her fuzzy hair flattened with sweat. She threw herself at the walls, kicked out at them, tried to climb up them.

Dad came back to check on her. "It's going to take her a while to get used to being without her mama." He gently wound one of Mary's braids around her head but said nothing more. After a bit he left and went to sit on the veranda.

Mary stood at the crack in the wall for two hours, murmuring and crooning, trying to soothe the young horse with her voice. When the filly finally collapsed, her long legs shaking, and folded into a heap in the straw, Mary opened the shed door and slipped inside. The yellow filly rolled her eyes as the girl crouched down beside her but didn't move to get up. Mary scratched the weanling's flat withers, asking to be her friend. The tiny whiskery muzzle touched her face, puffing soft air on her cheeks. Softly, Mary blew back into those sweetly curved nostrils.

The shed door creaked open and Mike pushed into the shed. The filly nickered and the pony huffed back. He sniffed the filly over and then, standing close, hung his head over the fuzzy yellow foal.

"You're not alone, little girl." Mary combed the wispy mane with her fingers. "We're going to stay right here with you."

"You got it wrong, Inglis." Simon Dalton's harsh voice jerked Mary back to the present. "I wasn't *giving* the filly away. I just wanted her out of sight. To get over the shock, you know."

"But you never asked after her. Not once," said Dad. "You never wanted to know what happened to her."

"For goodness' sakes, I'm a busy man. I have business concerns all over the world. I can't be expected to remember every little detail about all of them. That's why I hire good managers, to run things for me, to take care of the day-to-day matters."

"Reg Carson never did say anything to me," said Dad, referring to the old boss. "Not a single thing."

Henry broke in. "You know, it seems that everything's turned out very well, considering. The horse has gotten excellent care and training from Donny and young Mary here. And now the mare's a proven winner and a credit to your breeding."

"Yes, yes, thank you for that, Inglis. Mary, you too. I'll see you're both well paid for your time."

"I don't need to be paid!" Mary burst out. "Not for training my own horse."

"You can't take my sister's horse! She lives for that mare," said Tom.

"Now, Mary, Tom, you must realize this is a very valuable animal. Her mother cost me a great deal of money. Not to mention the expense of transporting her from Kentucky."

"But you didn't want her!" growled Tom.

"I just explained, that was all a misunderstanding. Mary, I will pay you and your father for looking after my horse all these years, but she still belongs to me."

"No, she doesn't! Colleen belongs with me. Everybody knows that!" Mary looked around at the faces surrounding her. They all knew it was true, that Colleen was hers. Why didn't someone speak up and say so?

Dalton puffed out his cheeks and sighed. "Mary, do you have a bill of sale for the mare? You don't, do you? That's because she was never signed over to you or your father. I'm a businessman, young lady. If I had wanted to give up my ownership of the animal, I would have completed all the necessary paperwork."

Diana Dalton tugged at his arm. "Simon, you're not really thinking of taking this girl's horse away from her, are you?"

Charlie Peters broke in. "Diana, horses with this much jumping ability are few and far between. That makes the mare worth a lot of money."

"But Mary rides her so well," said Dorothy.

"Does she?" Charlie shook his head. "You saw the trouble she had today controlling the mare."

"Yes, but with more training, more experience—"

"Dorothy, she's a *girl*. She'll never have the strength or stamina to make it around an international jumping course! And that's where this horse should be competing—at the very top. I've been searching high and low throughout this entire country for horses of this calibre. Believe me, I have found very few. And with the Stockholm Olympics just a year away, well, the pressure is on to find good mounts for our team."

Donny tore his hat from his head and pointed it at the ranch owner. "Dalton, you take that mare away from my girl and I'll quit. I won't spend another day on this ranch."

"Now, Inglis, calm down. We'll find Mary another horse, just as pretty."

"The horse belongs with Mary and you know it. Everybody on this ranch knows it! It doesn't matter whether she's got some piece of paper saying so; Colleen and Mary belong together."

"Now, Donny, please understand—" Charlie Peters began.

"Inglis to you!" flared Dad.

"All right, Mr. Inglis, let me explain the situation. I'm sure Mr. Dalton will agree to lend the mare—"

Mary cut in. "Her name is Colleen!"

"Yes, yes, *Colleen*. To continue, Simon will lend Colleen to the Canadian Equestrian Team to compete in the Olympics next year. And I'm certain that includes covering all of her expenses."

"Hold on there, Charlie," spluttered Simon Dalton.

"Simon, how good of you!" exclaimed his wife.

"Very generous indeed," agreed Dorothy.

Mary trembled all over. They were really going to do it, they were going to take Colleen away from her.

"Who's going to ride her?" Dad asked harshly.

"Why, Henry, of course," said Charlie.

"What!" said Henry. "This is the first I've heard about it."

"The team needs you," explained Charlie. "You're experienced and as cool as a cucumber under pressure. And you're very good at getting along with a hot-tempered horse."

"Don't worry, Henry, I'll give you the time off work," said Mr. Dalton.

"Listen, if you don't want to ride the mare, I'll find someone else who does," said Charlie. "You are my first choice, Henry, but there are other riders out there."

Henry bowed his head under the weight of the decision. "I'll ride her."

"This is the craziest thing I've ever heard," said Tom. "Mary should be riding that mare, no one else. Mr. Zee's never even sat on that horse's back."

"Mary *can't* ride, not in the Olympics," sighed Charlie Peters, his patience fraying. "We've gone over this before. She's too young and she's female. Women can't jump in the Games."

Mary was shaking so hard her teeth chattered. Beside her, Colleen pawed the grass. Mary began to lead the mare away.

"What are you doing?" asked Mr. Dalton.

"She's been standing long enough. I'm going to untack her," she stammered. A vague plan was forming in her head. She'd remove Colleen's saddle and change out of her riding clothes. Then she'd get some supplies from the house and, before anyone knew they were gone, ride away into the mountains with Colleen.

"I'll get someone to put her away. Slim! Come over here."

One of the ranch hands had been loitering nearby. "Yes, Mr. Dalton?"

"Take this mare into the horse barn and look after her. Make sure she's well taken care of."

"Will do. Mary, you're going to have to let go of those reins. Mary, please?"

"I can't, Slim. I can't let her go."

Slim looked over at Simon Dalton. "What am I supposed to do?"

"Mary, let go," her father told her brusquely.

"Dad, please..."

"She's not your horse, not anymore. You have to let her go."

"I can't," Mary whimpered. Her eyes were shut tight, her fingers clenched around the reins. She felt Colleen's soft muzzle press against her cheek, offering comfort. Warm air puffed on her skin. She was nearly empty inside, just a pounding heart, the rest of her body a hollow void.

Dad's strong fingers pried her hand open. She felt the leather straps pulled from her grasp, heard the whisper of crushed grass as Colleen was led away. Her heart thumped furiously, harder and harder, until...

17

Hush, hush, you're all right. Everything's going to be fine. You'll see, it will all work out in the end. I promise you.

A gentle hand rested on Mary's forehead, then smoothed her hair. She tried to open her eyes, saw a sliver of light, but the effort was too much. She let her lids fall shut again.

Shh. Shh, don't cry.

She heard the sound of soft weeping. Her eyes felt swollen and damp beneath their lids, and a trickle of something wet slid down her temple. A moment of pressure on her temple and the moisture was gone.

Rest now, Mary. I'll be nearby if you need me. Go to sleep, that's my girl.

A horse's whinny jerked Mary out of sleep. She threw the bedclothes aside and ran to her bedroom window. The floorboards were cool under her bare feet. Outside, droplets like dew glittered on the green grass of the home pasture, where the sprinkler had been spraying water all through the night.

A sorrel horse ran around the field, calling for his friends. He was the bright copper of a new penny, his flowing mane and tail the pale blond of wheat straw. A narrow white blaze ran down the centre of his face.

Dad and Tom and Dorothy hung over the pasture fence closest to the house, watching the new horse as he cantered around. Mary realized the horse was all by himself in the little field. She turned away from the window and hurried down the stairs and outside.

Tom saw her first. "Hey, look who's awake. Morning, sleepyhead."

"Where's Mike? Where is he? You didn't get rid of him, did you?"

Dad caught her by the shoulders. "Steady now, Mary. Don't get yourself all worked up again. Mike is just fine."

"Then where is he? Where's my pony?"

"Mary, he's gone down to the ranch yard," Dorothy explained in a gentle voice.

"Why? Mr. Dalton isn't going to take him away too, is he?"

"No, no, of course not. Oh, Mary!" Dorothy reached out to hug her, but Mary pulled away.

"Then why isn't he here? I want him back in his field where he belongs."

"Mary, he's gone down to keep Colleen company," said Dad. "We'll bring him back when she's settled in."

"When did he go? Why didn't anyone tell me?"

"Last night. You were sleeping, Mary. You've been asleep since yesterday noon. Guess you needed it."

Mary looked down at her pyjamas. Straggles of hair had come out of her braids, and her teeth felt fuzzy. Her stomach rumbled. She didn't care about feeding it, didn't care about washing or dressing. Colleen was gone.

The sorrel horse skidded to a stop before them. He stretched his neck over the fence, inspecting the small group.

"What's that horse doing in our field?" she asked.

"He's yours," Tom told her. "Mr. Dalton sent him over before he left."

"He's a good-looking horse, isn't he?" said Dorothy. Her blonde hair was gathered back into an untidy ponytail, and she still wore yesterday's dress. Dark circles underlined her eyes.

Mary remembered a hand on her forehead, a tissue pressed to her face to soak up tears. A lump rose in her throat. "He is. But I don't want him."

She broke away and started back to the house.

"Mary!" Dorothy called after her.

"Ma'am, just let her be," Dad said.

"But she's hurting so much."

"I know, but there's nothing we can do. Time is what she needs. Time heals a wound."

You're wrong, Dad. Some wounds never heal.

"When are we moving?" she asked that night at supper.

"I don't know, Mary," said Dad. "I haven't made up my mind about that."

"What do you mean? If you've quit, then we can't keep living here. This house comes with your job."

Dad and Tom looked at each other across the table.

"What? What's going on?" said Mary.

"Well, first things first, Miss Mary," said Dad. "Mr. Zee says not to worry, there's no rush for us to leave the house. So I guess I'll start looking around for another job, make sure I find a good one. After all, we don't want to move and find ourselves worse off than we are here."

Mary stabbed a green bean with her fork. "We aren't going anywhere, are we? We're staying right here."

"Dad just told you he's going to look around and see what kind of job he can find," said Tom.

"What about you? Are you looking around, too?"

Her brother shook his head. "I've got a good position on this ranch. Mr. Zee's a good boss. I like it here."

Mary understood they wouldn't be leaving the ranch. Dad had backed down from his threat to quit if Mr. Dalton took Colleen away. Oh, he'd pretend to try to find other work, but in the end they'd be staying put.

Part of her was outraged. Part of her wanted to have nothing at all to do with Simon Dalton, especially not living on his property, even though he rarely visited the ranch.

But another part of her was aware of Colleen close by on the ranch. Her heart ached at the notion of moving away and leaving her beloved friend behind.

"Finish up eating, Mary, so we can get the dishes done," said Tom. "It's been a long day and I'm tired."

She set her cutlery down on her plate.

"That's it? That's all you're going to eat?" asked Dad.

"I'm not hungry."

Her father rubbed his hand down his face. "Mary, I know this is a hard thing to take, but after a while it'll get a little easier."

Mary bent her head. She felt Dad's hand patting her shoulder. It didn't help. Nothing eased the pain that stabbed at her all day and night long. She was shattered, all her insides broken into sharp splinters that wouldn't quit pricking and scratching for a single moment.

Tom took her plate away and dumped the uneaten food into a pail for the neighbour's chickens. Dad's chair scraped against the floor as he got up. A moment later the screen door slammed.

A dishtowel landed on her shoulder. "Give me a hand with the washing up," said Tom.

When they were done, Mary made her way up the stairs to her room and dropped onto her bed. Outside, the rocking chair creaked on the veranda below. Through her open window she heard her father's voice.

"...shouldn't have gone away, Audrey. We need you, your girl needs you. Oh, Audrey, love, why'd you have to go and leave us?"

* * *

School started up. Early in the morning, Mary waited with the other ranch kids for the school bus. When it came, she climbed aboard and sat down in the seat right behind the driver where the bad kids sat. Nobody would bother her there.

In class she paid close attention to the lessons. If she kept her mind on other things, the pain inside her eased a bit. She knew she was letting Colleen down, forgetting about her like this, even for an hour or two, but the splinters had rubbed her raw. She had to make them stop, before they broke out through her skin.

One lunch hour, her teacher, Miss Johnson, held her back. "Mary, I've noticed how hard you're working this year and I'm very pleased. I'm sure your parents will be, too."

"There's only my dad."

"Oh, yes, that's right. Well, when he gets your report card, he'll be very proud of you." Miss Johnson gave her a bright smile. Then her face turned serious. "Are you feeling all right, Mary? You seem very tired, a little under the weather."

"I'm okay, miss."

Miss Johnson's eyebrows lifted. "Are you sure?"

"Yes, miss. I'm a bit tired, from all the homework."

"Well, your school work is certainly important, but you must get fresh air and sunshine, Mary. Promise me you'll go outside and have some fun?"

"I'll try, Miss Johnson." She looked away from the teacher's kind face. "May I go now?"

"Yes, of course, Mary. Go off with your friends. Winter's coming. Enjoy the warm weather while it's here."

18

"You're sure you don't mind me riding him?" asked Tom. He set his saddle on the woollen saddle blanket covering the sorrel's back and bent under the horse's barrel to catch hold of the cinch. The little horse stood like a rock while the string cinch was tightened around his girth.

"No, go ahead," said Mary. "He needs the exercise." She sat beside the pasture fence, her back resting against a post.

"That's right. So why haven't you been riding him?"

She shrugged. "I don't want to."

Her brother frowned, but he said nothing.

It wouldn't have mattered if he had. Mary no longer cared whether anyone was pleased with her or annoyed. If the people around her didn't like her behaviour, let them punish her. There wasn't anything else they could take away from her that she cared about losing, and she couldn't hurt any more than she already did.

Tom slipped the bit into the sorrel's mouth. He walked him for a minute, took the last few inches of slack out of the cinch and swung aboard. The red horse didn't move a foot as Tom gently settled into the saddle.

He guided the horse on a long-reined walk around the field a few times before jogging and loping. "He's got a real nice handle on him," he called to Mary, circling the sorrel in a figure eight. He galloped up to his sister and leaned back. The sorrel slid to a stop. "He's a nice horse. Come on, try him out."

She shook her head.

"He feels real powerful. I'll bet he could be a jumper, if you taught him." Tom sighed when Mary didn't respond. "So, what are you going to call him?"

"I don't know."

"He's got to have a name."

"You name him."

"All right, then, I will. I'll call him Red." Tom grinned, waiting for his sister's protests at such an ordinary name for the flashy horse.

"Sure, whatever you want." Mary shrugged.

"Okay, Red it is. Mary, are you going to mope around like this forever?"

While he was waiting for an answer, a car drove up and parked beside the house.

"Looks like we've got company," said Tom.

The driver's door swung open and a woman got out. She walked slowly to the house, looking around as if she wasn't sure she was at the right place. The screen door banged shut behind Dad as he came out of the house and onto the veranda.

"That's my teacher," said Mary. "That's Miss Johnson."

"Why did she come here," said Tom, "on a Saturday afternoon? Let me out, Mary. I'm going to say hi."

Mary opened the gate and Tom rode Red through into the yard. She shut the gate and ducked down behind a wild rose bush growing along the fenceline. Peering through the branches, she had a clear view of the house. She heard Tom call out a greeting as he rode up to Dad and Miss Johnson, standing side by side on the veranda. Then she heard Dad shouting her name.

"I'll get her," said Tom, turning Red around.

Hunkered down low, Mary hurried along the fence. On the other side of the house, she slipped through the rails and darted across the dirt road into the brush. Seconds later, hooves clomped on the hardpan.

"Mary? Mary, come here," called Tom. "Dad wants you." He waited a few moments before riding back to the house.

Mary stayed still while the hoofbeats died away. Then she pushed through the saplings and brush until she was on a narrow path. She followed it all the way to the ranch yard.

This close to October, the late afternoons cooled off quickly. Mary shivered as the sun slid down through the sky to the mountains. In the big barn, she discovered a slicker draped over a stall door and shrugged it on. Then she scurried from building to building, making her way, as she had done every day for the past two weeks, through the ranch yard and up the short incline to the big house and the paddocks beyond.

Colleen was waiting for her. She stood at the fence, as still as a golden statue in the falling sun. Catching sight of Mary, she whinnied, instantly recognizing her lifelong friend and partner, even decked out in a man's oilskin slicker.

"Hush, Colleen, hush now." Mary wrapped her arms around the mare's neck and pressed her face into her mane. With winter coming on, Colleen's coat was changing from the smooth slickness of silk to the soft fuzz of a late summer peach. Mary felt Colleen's windpipe expand against the muscles of her upper arm as the mare took a deep breath. Mary filled her own lungs with air and held it, waiting until Colleen exhaled before she let go. The dull ache in her chest eased off, just a little—the only peace she felt these days.

A nose bunted at her pockets. Mary opened her eyes to grin at the grey pony. "Hi, Mike. No, I didn't bring you a treat. Next time, I promise."

Mike swished his tail and returned to his grazing.

"Hello, Mary."

Mary dropped her arms and spun around. Henry Zelinski leaned up against the open door of the little stable. She began to walk away quickly.

"Where are you going?" he asked.

"I know I shouldn't be here. I'm sorry. I'll go right away."

"Henry, what are you doing just standing..."

Dorothy came out of the stable. "Mary! Oh, how lovely to see you."

"I'm going."

"No, don't! Please, stay."

"I can't."

"Why not?" asked Henry. "Why can't you stay?"

"Because...I just can't."

"That's too bad. Because Colleen's been doing a lot better lately. She's eating better and putting on weight. We thought you were probably the reason."

"You knew? You knew I was coming here?"

Henry nodded. "With Colleen standing at the fence at four o'clock every afternoon, watching the road, it wasn't hard to figure out what was going on. Then Dorothy saw you and we knew for sure."

"I had to see her." Mary hung her head. "I had to be with her."

Dorothy put her arm around Mary. "Of course you did. And she needs to be with you."

"But she doesn't belong to me anymore."

"She does, Mary. The bond between you and Colleen will always be there."

"But Mr. Dalton owns her! He decides what happens to her. He could take her away! And then...then I would never see her again." She pulled away from Dorothy.

"Mary, listen to me," said Henry. "I give you my promise I will do everything I can to make sure that never happens."

"How can you promise that? You don't own Colleen."

"No, I don't, but I will do whatever I can to influence Simon Dalton to leave Colleen here on the ranch in my care. She'll still be near you, Mary."

"If Mr. Dalton listens to you, then tell him to give her back to me."

Henry shook his head sadly. "Mary, I tried, but the mare is simply too valuable."

"I wish I'd never taken Colleen to the PNE. We should have just stayed here on the ranch, stayed right where we were, where we'd always been. She could have stayed an ordinary horse and nobody would have wanted her but me."

"Mary, I can't tell you how sorry we are that things have turned out this way," said Dorothy. "You know you can come over and see Colleen any time you want, don't you? And you don't have to hide from us."

Mary nodded wordlessly. As hard as it was to see her beloved horse in someone else's pasture, it would be even harder not to see her at all.

"You know, if we got a move on we could fit a ride in before dark," said Henry. "What do you think, ladies?"

"That's a marvellous idea," said Dorothy.

"Well, Mary, what about you? Are you coming riding?"

Mary stared at Henry. Her eyes slid to Colleen, wondering if he could possibly mean...

"Yes, on Colleen. Simon Dalton may be her owner

now, but he's left her care and training completely up to me. So if you could help me out by exercising her, I'd really appreciate it. Because, as you know, Colleen needs a lot of exercising."

"I…I haven't got my riding clothes on."

"Hurry home and change. We'll get the horses ready. Don't worry, we'll wait for you," laughed Dorothy as Mary rushed off.

"Hi, Dad. Hello, Miss Johnson."

Dad and her teacher had been so busy talking they hadn't seen her coming. She bounded up the stairs onto the veranda and charged through the door into the house. "Be right back."

Upstairs in her room, her father's voice drifted up to her in a lilting rhythm, punctuated by giggles from Miss Johnson. Mary pulled on her jodhpurs, hand-me-downs from Dorothy, and a pair of knee-high socks. She tugged a lightweight wool sweater over her head and brushed the snarls from her hair so she could swiftly weave it into two braids. Slip feet into jodhpur boots, cram helmet on head and she was ready. Oh, wait, better wear gloves, more hand-me-downs. Colleen was sure to pull on the reins.

She clattered down the stairs and burst outside.

"Hold your horses! Where are you off to in such a hurry?" asked Dad.

She skidded to a stop. Dad was tipped back in the rocking chair, grinning like a boy. Miss Johnson had a similar smile on her face.

"I'm going riding. With the Zees. Dad, I'm going to ride Colleen! Bye, Miss Johnson! Nice to see you."

"Good to see you, too, Mary," said her teacher.

"Be home in time for supper," her father called after her.

She waved to show she'd heard.

"Well, there can't be anything wrong with a girl who's got that kind of energy," she heard Catherine Johnson say as she jogged off in the direction of the big house. "Now, I wonder, would you like any help getting supper ready?"

19

"The Royal Winter Fair has one of the most prominent horse shows in the whole country," said Dorothy. "Riders come from all over North America, and even Britain and Europe, to compete in it. And with the Olympic equestrian events being held next year in Stockholm, well, this year's Royal is even more important. Charlie Peters and the other selectors will be there, watching how the riders perform, before they decide who will be on the Canadian team."

"So you want to take Mary along with you? Not to compete, just to keep the horse happy. No, Tom, you stay sitting. I'll give Catherine a hand washing up." Dad got up and joined Miss Johnson, who was already at the sink. This was her sixth Saturday-night family supper, and she'd been pitching in with the cleanup right from the start.

"Yes, Donny, we'd like Mary to come with us," said Dorothy. "Colleen is a lot more settled in her care."

"We'll be away for about three weeks," said Henry. "Five days by train getting to Toronto, then a few days to settle in before the jumping competition begins.

After that, a day of rest and then home again. Mr. Dalton will, of course, pay for everything."

Mary crossed her fingers under the kitchen table. *Please, Dad, please say yes.*

Dad turned around, leaning against the counter, towel in hand. "What's included in everything?"

"Hotel rooms, meals, entrance fees."

"My goodness, that's very generous of him," said Miss Johnson. "This jumping competition must be very important to him."

"That's a long way for a young girl to go," said Dad, "without her family."

Henry twisted around in his chair to face Donny Inglis. "I've talked to Joe and he says he can spare Tom. Dalton will pay him his regular wages, plus his expenses. That is, if it's all right by you."

"Tom's a young man now, earns his own living. So I guess he's able to make up his own mind."

"Yes, sir, I'll come to Toronto," said Tom.

"Mary would be missing a lot of school days," said Dad. He looked at Miss Johnson, who smiled back at him.

"I could prepare homework to send along with her," said Miss Johnson. "She's been doing so well this year, I'm sure she'll have no problem catching up. And I'd be happy to help her."

"That's kind of you, Catherine."

"My pleasure." Miss Johnson turned back to the sink, but not before Mary could see that her cheeks were flushed.

"All right, then, Mary, you can go to Toronto. If that's what you want." Dad frowned in concern as he studied his daughter. "It'll be hard for you, won't it? Because you should be...well, you should be the one riding her. Sorry, Mr. Zee. I don't mean to offend you, but there it is, right out in the open."

Mary nodded. "I have to do it, Dad, because Colleen needs me. It wouldn't be right for her to travel all that way without a friend."

"All the way to Toronto. That's a long way for my little girl to go."

Miss Johnson reached out to gently touch his hand.

"So, we're all set." Henry set his clasped hands on the table with a heavy sigh. "I just want to say I'm sorry about the way things have turned out. I wanted to help Mary become a better rider, the way my father helped me. I thought I was giving her an opportunity, but I was wrong. I'm very sorry," he repeated.

Dad shook his head. "I've got to shoulder my share of the blame. I should have told Mr. Dalton what I'd done and settled things while the horse was still a filly. But all that's water under the bridge. We're moving on, eh, Miss Mary?"

Mary pursed her lips and nodded. Dad was sorry, Mr. Zelinski was sorry, even Dorothy was sorry for saying aloud the words that had started this whole mess. Now Mary had to be content with riding her partner around the ranch and caring for her in the stable. The thrills of competition, a glorious future with her golden mare where anything—everything!—was possible...that had just been dreams, made-up stuff. Now she was back in the real world, living a real life. And life was tough, everyone said so. She had to toughen up and get on with it.

And forget she'd ever dreamed of anything else.

* * *

Five days of travel. At first Mary sat transfixed at the train window, gazing in awe at the stark majesty of the Rocky Mountains and then the thick, dark forests of the foothills, which gave way to an endless wind-blown sea of dun-coloured prairie, stretching out to join the horizon with nothing in between. All her life, Mary had been surrounded by mountains and hills. Their treed slopes shouldered aside the wind; their valleys offered rich lands and winding rivers. In contrast, all this wide open space was bewildering. How did anyone find her way in a land without features under a sky so huge?

"Mary, could you please be still?" asked Dorothy, flipping the page of her book.

"I'll try." She'd never been inside for so many days. And nights, because they slept on the train too, in bunks in the sleeper cars.

"Shouldn't you be doing school work?"

"I'm already halfway through the exercises Miss

Johnson assigned. There's some reading, but I can't seem to—" Mary bounced on her seat.

"Settle down?" Dorothy suggested wryly.

"Whoops. Sorry."

Dorothy sighed. She looked up as her husband marched past along the narrow aisle. "Henry, where are you going?"

"To check on the horse."

"Another one who can't sit still. Go with him, Mary. Go see your mare."

Dorothy returned to her book without noticing her mistake.

Henry led the way through the passenger cars to the freight car close behind the engine. The car had ten loose boxes, big enough for the horses to turn around or lie down. As soon as Mary stepped through the door, Colleen nickered. Tom looked up from where he sat on a hay bale outside her stall, reading a book. "Back again?"

"A man can only take so many naps in a day," said Henry. He sat down beside Tom.

The loose boxes were filled with animals en route to the fair. Like Tom, their grooms and caretakers sat on bales of hay, swapping stories or napping. Mary went around and greeted each animal: the teams of Clydesdales, the Morgan stallion with the impossibly long mane and tail, the white-headed Hereford bulls, and the sloe-eyed Jersey cows, their gleaming butterscotch coats nearly matching Colleen's. All of them the best of the best, the most superb examples of western livestock, fed, groomed and exercised into perfect condition, on their way to compete with their eastern cousins.

And Colleen was among their number.

"Well now, Miss Mary, your brother's been telling us quite the story," said the Clydesdales' groom. "He says you can ride that palomino there over jumps higher than a man's head."

"It's true, I can."

"My oh my, that'd be something to see. I'll have to come and watch you at the Royal."

"You can't. I mean, I'm not riding her in the show. Mr. Zee is."

The man nodded, thinking he understood. "Those jumps are big. It's a dangerous sport, even for a man."

"That's not it," said Mary. "That's not why I'm not riding."

The man waited for her to explain, but she said no more.

* * *

Lakes began to appear outside the train window. Rocky outcrops sprang up in between stands of evergreen brush. Islands dotted the lakes, and cabins clustered their shores, windows and doors shut tight for winter. Huge oceans of water appeared—the Great Lakes. The train rolled through farmland, enormous hip-roofed barns standing guard over fields of turned-over dark soil, frost riming the edges of the ploughs. Mary admired the double-storeyed houses of brick or stone, their tall windows glowing with light against the late afternoon dusk.

"Look, Mary, there it is. The city." Dorothy pointed out the window to another ocean in the distance, this one of sparkling lights spreading out to reach the dark horizon.

"All of it? All those lights? That's all one city? It must be so big."

"It is," said Dorothy. "It's like nothing you've ever seen before."

Charlie Peters met them at the train station with his car and a horse trailer. He organized their luggage while Tom and Henry unloaded Colleen from the train and led her onto the trailer.

"Everyone ready?" Charlie asked once they were all in the car. "All right, then, let's go. We're off to the Royal!"

For all the glamour and prestige of the Royal Winter Fair, its stabling was cramped and crowded. There was a bed in a dormitory for Tom, but Mary was expected to stay with the Zelinskis in Charlie Peters' home.

"The Daltons are having a few people over on Saturday," he said, ushering his guests through the front door. "You're invited, of course."

"Sorry, Charlie, no can do. The Puissance is held that evening," said Henry.

"I realize that. This will be in the late afternoon, more of a tea party. Some very influential people will be coming. You and Dorothy really should be there. There will be plenty of time for you to get to the stable. I'm sure your groom here will have your horse ready to go."

"Charlie, Mary isn't our groom," said Dorothy. "She's more of a guest."

"I'm sorry. My mistake. I understood the young lady was here to help with the mare."

"She is, but she's not a groom. Not really. Let's just call Mary our friend."

Charlie's house was large and rambling, with rooms on three floors. Mary's was on the top storey. Peering out the window, she thought she could see the Canadian National Exhibition grounds, where the Royal Winter Fair was held. Not too far to walk if that was the only way to get there. She planned on spending every moment she could at the Royal with Colleen.

After a late supper she left the adults chatting and went upstairs to her room. She lay in bed, her head filled to overflowing with new sights and sounds. She thought of Tom, back at the stable, topping up Colleen's water bucket before shaking out a flake or two of hay in the corner of her stall. She'd never been so far from both her brother and her father before in her life.

Was Dad lonely with both of them gone? She recalled how his eyes crinkled in the corners from smiling every time he looked at Miss Johnson. Catherine, he called her. And Miss Johnson looked so much younger when she tilted her head to look up at Dad. She was a pretty lady and so very kind.

Drifting off to sleep, Mary's mind filled with the image of a pair of golden ears rising up before her, higher and higher until they were soaring above the earth and into the stars of the night sky.

20

"Look, Tom, have you ever seen anything like that in your entire life?" asked Mary.

"Never." Tom shook his head in wonder. "I never have. Look at them all, dressed to the nines like this was some sort of royal occasion."

"But it is. It's the Royal Winter Fair."

They were at the in-gate of the enclosed ring where the evening's jumping competition was scheduled. Even now the ring crew was putting the finishing touches on the course, arranging pots of shrubbery beside the jumps, draping garlands of flowers over the jump standards. Under the bright lights, the jump ring glowed with colour, a fitting complement to the occasion.

For it *was* an occasion and a very important one, judging by the crowd filling the stands. Dressed as if they were going to a ball, the women wore long evening gowns under fur coats, their hair pinned up on top of their heads to display necks and ears glittering with diamonds and sapphires. The men were decked out in black tuxedo suits with long split tails behind and cut low in front to display snowy white shirt fronts.

"They look like penguins," said Tom. "Now why would a grown man let himself be dressed up like a bird?"

"Same reason he'd wear a big hat and a neckerchief," said Mary, eyeing her brother's cowboy hat.

Tom frowned and pushed his black felt hat down on his head. "I wear this hat for a reason. It keeps the sun out of my eyes and the rain off my neck."

"Guess what, Tom? The sun isn't shining in here and it's not raining."

Tom pretended to scowl at his sister's teasing. "Never know when it might rain. Big roof like this one could spring a leak any moment."

"But it would still have to be raining outside. Come on, let's see if Mr. Zee needs us."

They made their way through the busy warm-up area over to where Henry Zelinski was riding Colleen in circles. The palomino was on her toes, dancing sideways with barely contained excitement.

"She knows what's up," said Tom.

Mary took an extra breath to ease the stab of jealousy she felt. "The ring crew is just about finished," she reported. "The course should be open for walking any minute now."

Mr. Zelinski kicked his feet free of the stirrups and vaulted from the saddle. He ran up the irons and lifted the reins over Colleen's head. Before he handed them to Tom, he ran his hand down the mare's white blaze. "Not long now, my lady."

Colleen shook off his hand and stamped a front foot. Mary bit her lip to hide her smile. She stroked the mare's neck and felt her quieten under her touch.

Mr. Zelinski shrugged and went off to walk the course.

Colleen was far down the order of go, close to the end. In spite of Mary's soothing, the mare had worked herself into a lather before it was her turn to jump.

"She's got herself in a bit of a state, hmm?" said Charlie Peters as Henry rode Colleen past him to the in-gate. "Well, she's young. A few rounds with an experienced rider aboard, that's what she needs."

A cheer greeted the announcement of Henry Zelinski's name as he entered the ring.

"Good to see you back, Zelinski!" someone shouted from the stands.

"Come on!" Tom shouldered his way to the gate, towing Mary along with him. They squeezed into the small crowd gathered to watch. "This is the best we're going to do."

The spectators had overflowed the stands and spilled out onto the stairways. Mary saw Henry look up at the ceiling. She craned her neck back and saw young men sitting on the rafters overhead, their feet dangling.

The whistle blew to begin. From the moment she lunged into canter, it was obvious Colleen was barely under control. She bolted at the first jump, throwing herself into the air a full stride away. Landing with a shake of her head and a buck, she charged toward the next jump, a very solid oxer.

Mary clutched Tom's sleeve. "She's going too fast. He's got to slow her down."

"I don't think he can," said Tom grimly.

A hush fell over the crowd. Henry's face was a frozen mask of self-control. Only the tight set of his jaw betrayed his struggle to retain control of the impetuous animal underneath him. Colleen flung her head back and forth, resisting his attempts to slow her pace, only focusing on the enormous jumps in her path at the last possible moment, when she flung her body over and jerked her legs out of the way.

Henry leaned back and took a firm hold as they turned to the in and out.

Pay attention! Mary urged Colleen silently. *There are two jumps and only one stride between them!*

Colleen leaned against the bit and stood off the first jump as if she were racing in the Grand National steeplechase. The huge leap took her well past the fence. Now she had to shorten, compress her body to fit in one small stride before leaving the ground again, this time to clear an impossibly wide oxer.

Henry's elbows were bent past his body as he struggled to rein the mare in. Throwing her head violently, Colleen stretched her front legs forward, reaching with her long stride until her hooves were nearly under the front rails of the jump before her.

She was too close, much too close. It was impossible to clear the jump now.

She tried.

Contorting her body, Colleen reared back, shifting a thousand pounds of body weight onto her two back legs. She sprang up, folding her knees above her chest, her long neck reaching above the double rails of the oxer. Her head cleared the fence, then her neck and shoulders. Her girth, with Henry folded tight to the withers, hovered over the second rail as she strained to lift her hind legs clear of the first.

Mary sighed, relieved, as the back hooves skimmed over the top of the rail. Colleen's front legs unfolded, preparing for landing.

From a distance it was impossible to see one rear hoof dropping down just an inch on the wrong side of the back rail. Trapped between the mare's back feet, the pole toppled from its cups. Colleen landed on her front hooves, her neck outstretched for balance, and swung her back feet under her body.

Except she couldn't. The jump rail was still between them, a hoof on each side. Twisting her body, she landed one foot, but the other came down on top of the rail and buckled over. Colleen staggered, falling to her knees. Henry tumbled over her shoulder to the ground and lay still.

For one long awful moment the entire building was silent.

"Son of a gun!" Tom pushed through the gate and

ran toward Henry. Mary hurried after him. By the time she reached him, Henry was on his hands and knees.

"Got the wind knocked out of me," he puffed.

"Let me give you a hand, sir." Tom helped Henry to his feet. He tugged off his neckerchief and held it out. "For your face."

"Thanks." Henry swiped the dirt off his face. "Is the mare all right?"

They looked around. Colleen was dashing about the ring, leading the ring crew on a merry chase.

"She looks just fine, Mr. Zee," said Tom.

"Mary, go catch your mare," said Henry.

"Colleen! Colleen!" Mary put two fingers in her mouth and whistled.

Colleen froze. A man made a grab at the reins. Jerking her head away, the mare trotted across the ring, dodging the jumps until she reached Mary.

The mare bowed her head until her forehead was resting against the girl's. "Come on, Colleen, the show's over for you tonight."

Side by side the golden horse and the dark-haired girl walked across the ring to the exit, leaving the applause of the crowd behind them.

As Charlie Peters drove them home, Mary leaned her head against the window in the back seat of the big car and pretended to be asleep. Through half-opened eyes, she watched the city streets fly past. Even this late at night there was still traffic. The street lamps shone down on groups of people walking home from the horse show.

It had been hard seeing Colleen jump without her. Watching from behind the gate, jealousy burning bitter in her throat, she'd ridden every single jump in her head. Including the fall. In that moment, Mary had only cared for the safety of her beloved friend.

"You've got your work cut out for you with that mare, Henry," said Charlie. "Ah well, you'll soon get her sorted out. She's not a ladies' mount, that's for sure."

"I think Mary did a fine job with her," Dorothy said stoutly.

"Oh, she did, she did. My hat's off to you, Mary, for getting her this far."

"She's still very new to competition," said Henry. "She'll settle down as the week goes on. And she needs more exercise."

"I met up with a fellow tonight who's got a few nice horses at his farm an hour or so from the city," said Charlie. "Told him we'd come by first thing in the morning and try them out. Well, I suppose we can go after you ride."

"Will that leave you enough time?" asked Dorothy. "You don't want to be late for tomorrow night's class."

"Mary? Mary, are you awake?"

It took her a moment to realize Henry was speaking to her. "Oh! Yes, I am."

"Perhaps you could ride Colleen for me…"

Outside the car the street lamps were spinning in a blur of light. Or was it the car going around and around?

Then she heard the rest of Henry's sentence. "…tomorrow morning. Just exercise her. Lots of trotting to get any stiffness out. If you wouldn't mind."

"Sure. I can do that." *Idiot! Did you really think he was asking you to jump her tomorrow night in the show?*

She had. For one perfect, shining moment she had. And in those brief seconds she realized just how very much she wanted to.

"If Mary exercises Colleen, we can get away on time," said Henry.

"Are you sure that's a good idea?" asked Charlie. "After tonight—"

"I'm sure," replied Henry. "Absolutely sure."

21

"You should be the one riding her tonight," grumbled Tom. He set the saddle on Colleen's back. "Mr. Zee is a good rider, but Colleen jumps better with you. Any fool can see that."

"Tom, shh. Don't talk like that," scolded Mary.

"Why not? Why can't I say what I think?"

"Because it doesn't do any good. It doesn't change anything, not one bit."

"Old Dalton and this Charlie Peters think they know best, but they're wrong."

"But they're the ones in charge." Mary slid the bridle over Colleen's head and fastened the buckles.

"What's wrong with you? It's not like you to give up so easy."

"What am I supposed to do, Tom? If you know, tell me."

Tom shrugged. "Mary, I haven't got a clue."

"I don't either, Tom. I just don't know what I can do that would change their minds. Give me a leg up, will you? Colleen's tired of standing around."

After trotting a few circuits of the warm-up ring, Mary realized how much Colleen had changed. While the mare fought against Henry's very controlled riding style in the show ring, she'd learned a lot from his training methods. She was more responsive to Mary's requests. There was a steady, relaxed rhythm to her paces. Without ever appearing to do much of anything, Henry had improved the mare's training more in a couple of months than Mary had done in several years.

He knows a lot about riding and training horses, she reminded herself. *But I know about Colleen. Why won't they listen to me?*

She was alert to any signs that Colleen had been frightened by the fall to her knees the night before. Nothing like that had ever happened to the mare before. But she didn't seem bothered at all. Her stride was free and steady. In fact, the more she moved, trotting around the ring lap after lap, the more she relaxed. Colleen was a high-spirited horse. Even after the long train trip, she had energy to burn.

Then, outside the ring, a man dropped his show program. Colleen jumped sideways at the sudden motion. In an instant, her new training was forgotten. She locked her neck and bolted across the ring, banging into a heavyweight hunter. The big horse grunted at the impact but stood firm. Mary seized the chance and turned the mare in a tight circle to regain control.

"I'm sorry," she called.

"No harm done, miss. You're all right?" asked the hunter's rider.

She nodded.

"That's a lot of horse, a real handful. Maybe a bit too much for a young girl like you, eh?"

"I can manage her just fine, thank you!" she snapped.

"Well, there's no need to be rude."

"Sorry," she said, but the other rider had already ridden off.

Mary gritted her teeth in frustration. *One day,* she vowed, *one day I'll show you.*

By the time Mary returned Colleen to her stall, Tom had it cleaned and ready for her with fresh hay and clean water. After Mary untacked, he brushed the mare down and picked her feet. Colleen sighed contentedly and dove into her feed.

When they had put everything away, Tom pulled out a program. "Did you know the Royal Winter Fair is the biggest indoor fair in the whole world?"

Mary shook her head. She'd been so caught up in the horse show, she'd forgotten about the rest of the fair.

"Well, it is. And I think you and I should go have a look at it. Come on, Mary, I'll treat you to a corn dog."

It took several days to fully explore the huge complex of buildings housing all the exhibits and animals. Mary returned to the Horse Palace late every afternoon, weary and footsore from traipsing through exhibit halls and barns.

The exercise helped relieve some of her anxiety over Colleen's jumping performance. As the week went on, the mare was slowly giving in to Henry's control. But her attitude was sullen and her jumping mechanical. Mary watched in bewilderment as the mare who would once twist and contort her legs and body rather than touch a rail was suddenly knocking two or three or four to the ground every round.

"Just one tonight. That's an improvement," Charlie Peters told Simon Dalton when he arrived to watch his new horse after a few days away. "She's inexperienced when it comes to competition. She needed a little time to settle in but it's getting better. She should be in good form for the weekend."

Mary, overhearing, didn't think nine knockdowns and a refusal in four classes were much of an improvement, not from a mare who'd never brought down a rail in her life until now, but she said nothing. What was the sense in speaking up? They wouldn't listen to her, not these important men who believed they knew so much more than anyone else, especially a fourteen-year-old girl.

She kept on riding Colleen early every morning for exercise. Henry said he needed the extra sleep.

"Which is strange, when you think about it," said Tom. "He's up and out on the job by five o'clock on the ranch."

"Maybe it's because of the time change. We're three hours ahead here," said Mary.

"Or maybe he just wants you to ride Colleen. Maybe he realizes Colleen settles down when you ride her."

"Do you really think so, Tom?"

"Yes, I do. The mare's happier with you, any idiot can see that. And Mr. Zee's no idiot."

"Oh, I wish..." Mary closed her eyes.

"What? What do you wish?"

"I wish he'd let me ride her in the show. Just once, here at the Royal. I'd show them. I'd show them all."

"I know you would. But Mr. Zee isn't in charge. It's not up to him."

22

"Mary, Tom, could I speak with you for a moment?" asked Henry Zelinski.

"Sure, Mr. Zee. Oh, afternoon, Mrs. Zee," said Tom. "What's up?"

Mary came out of Colleen's stall, body brush in hand.

"Tonight's the Puissance," Henry began.

Tom's forehead creased. "Pwee-sawnz? What's that?"

"The high-jump class," explained Dorothy.

"So why isn't it called that?"

"Because it's got to have a French name," said Mary.

"Would you two please listen?" Henry said sharply. "Dorothy and I have to go to the Daltons' house before the class. Some silly get-together with a bunch of stuffed shirts that Simon Dalton has arranged." He rolled his eyes. "We should be back in time but, just in case, I'd like you to have Colleen tacked up and ready to go, Tom."

"Will do."

"And Mary, I'll need you to warm her up. Take a few practice fences. Not too many; she'll do plenty of jumping in the ring."

"You want me to jump her?"

"Isn't that what I just said?"

"Henry, that was rude!" said Dorothy.

"I know." He took a deep breath. "I'm sorry, Mary, for being so irritable. I've got a lot on my mind right now."

"He's an absolute grouch! He doesn't want to go to the Daltons' but Simon insists." Dorothy glanced at her watch. "Henry, we'd better go back to the house and get ready."

"Yes, yes, of course. There's just one more thing. Tom, would you come with me to the show office?"

"Okay, but what for?"

"Nothing too serious. Just a form that needs to be signed. For Mary. She needs a...a permission slip to ride in the warm-up ring tonight. Since you're eighteen you can sign it for her. Mary, you don't need to bother coming with us. Stay here and keep Colleen company."

"Bye, Mr. and Mrs. Zee. Have a good time tonight," said Mary. "And don't worry, I'll have Colleen ready."

Henry turned back. "Oh, and Mary, be sure to wear your good riding clothes. It's an important class. You'll need to be properly turned out."

"But I'm just going to be in the warm-up area," said Mary to Colleen when they were alone. "No one in the audience is going to see me back there. Well, that's Mr. Zee for you—a real stickler for details."

It was early evening. Mary watched the ring crew set a row of wood blocks along the top of the wall placed in the centre of the ring. The jump was constructed of sturdy wood planks painted to look exactly like a red brick wall. Rows and rows of extra wood "bricks" waited nearby on a wagon. Each horse and rider that cleared the wall would go on to the next round. And each round began with the jump crew raising the height of the wall another row of bricks. The competition would go on until only one horse had jumped clear.

The stands were full to overflowing. Mary tipped her head back and saw the rafter seats had been claimed. The atmosphere in the coliseum crackled with excitement and anticipation. She shivered, feeling a buzz of electricity.

She turned and jogged back to Tom and Colleen, her ankles stiff in her tall black boots. "The class is going to start any minute now. Where is he?"

"Don't know," shrugged Tom.

Mary bounced on her toes. "He's going to be late! Do you think I should tell the whipper-in?"

"Good idea, but let me do it. I'll get him to put Colleen near the end of the class. Here, you hold her." He pushed the mare's reins into Mary's hands.

He was gone for a long time. "All settled," he said on his return. He didn't stay long. "There's one more thing I've got to do. Be right back!"

Thank goodness Tom was staying calm. Mary was so anxious her teeth were chattering. What had happened to Mr. Zee? Why was he so late? She peered through the shifting bodies all around her, hoping to see his lean horseman's frame striding toward her. She caught a glimpse of a familiar face but it was Tom, ducking through the throng, carrying something in his arms. As he drew close, she saw he was grinning. Mary sighed in relief.

"He's here, right? He made it!"

"Who?" asked Tom.

"Mr. Zee, of course!"

"No, he's not here."

"Tom, this is terrible. How can you smile like that?"

Tom held out his arms. Mary saw he had a black riding coat and a velvet-covered helmet. "What's that?"

"Your riding coat, mademoiselle. And your helmet." Tom tugged a length of white silk from his neck and bowed. "As well, your stock tie. The pin is in my pocket. Hurry up, put it on."

"Are you crazy? I can't ride Colleen. Mr. Zee will kill me."

Tom shook his head, grinning. "It's okay, Mary. Hurry, get dressed. The class is starting."

"No, Tom, I can't. You don't understand. Mr. Zee needs to jump Colleen here to get back on the national team. Late or not, he's not going to let me ride her."

Tom's grin stretched wider. "Mary, he is. This is his idea."

"What are you talking about?"

"Mr. Zee took me to the show office this afternoon

so I could sign for you to ride tonight. Hey, are you okay?" He caught his sister by the shoulder to hold her steady. "Take a deep breath, Mary, that's it. And another. Better now?"

She nodded. "I can't believe it. Mr. Zee is letting me ride?"

"That's right. Now will you get a move on?"

"But what about trying out for the national team?"

"Mary, I don't know about any of that stuff. Nothing else matters right now but you putting on this silly bow tie and suit jacket, then getting up on that horse of yours and into the ring."

"Yes, yes, you're right." Fingers fumbling, Mary knotted the stock tie around her neck and fastened it in place with the long pin Tom dug out of his pocket. Then she shrugged on the black coat. Her hair hung in two long braids down her back.

Like a child's, she thought. Then she realized she *was* a child. She wasn't yet fifteen.

Tom legged her up into Colleen's saddle. Mary slipped her feet into the irons with a sigh. This was home.

She walked Colleen around the warm-up ring. There were only a few horses left in the first round, including Colleen. Already a number of horses had left the area and gone back to their stalls after failing to jump clear over the wall.

The hurried tattoo of Mary's heart had been replaced by a slower, powerful rhythm that sent the blood flowing to every cell of her body. She was with Colleen. Trust and confidence flowed back and forth between them.

There was no course plan to learn. The strategy was simple. One solidly built jump in the middle of the ring with an optional warm-up fence off to the side. If they got over the wall without knocking down any of the bricks, they went on to the next round.

"Number fifty-five!" shouted the whipper-in.

"Right here," said Mary, moving Colleen up to the in-gate.

The stout bay in the ring was approaching the warm-up fence. He bounced over it and headed for the wall. His rider leaned back, checking the bay's headlong gallop. The horse pushed off his powerful quarters and heaved his bulk into the air and over the wall. He landed with a grunt to the cheers and whistles of the crowd, his rider patting his thick neck over and over.

The whipper-in opened the gate. "You're on," he told Mary, and she sent Colleen into the ring.

The bay horse passed close by on his way out, towering over Colleen as if she were a pony. Mary heard the announcer say Colleen's name, then nothing more. The whole world had shrunk to an oval ring, a red brick wall and the golden mare beneath her. She thought *canter* and Colleen moved into the gait with the grace of a gazelle.

It felt like Colleen was skipping over the ground, energy building with every step she took. Her slender ears turned forward, tuning in on the wall. Her head rose and Mary felt the mare's quarters begin to crouch lower and lower. She held the reins loosely in her hands, kept the pressure of her legs light. Colleen had the situation summed up perfectly. She knew exactly what to do.

The silver mane brushed Mary's chin as the mare's neck rose up before her. A sudden surge and they were in the air, arcing over the breadth of the wall. The applause of the crowd told her they were clear. A soft bump of landing and they were cantering again, on the far side of the wall now, Colleen breathing light and easy as if she'd hardly made an effort.

She shook her head against Mary's request to pull up. Her thin ears flicked back and forth. *Where are the rest of the jumps?* they seemed to say. *Come on, I'm ready to go!*

"That's it," Mary told her. "Just the one. But we'll be back."

And they were, round after round. The wall grew higher and higher. The ring crew was busy now, replacing the wood bricks as horse after horse failed to clear the obstacle and knocked them to the ground. But not every horse. Cheers roared out of the crowd as a long-limbed chestnut stretched over the wall. Then a sturdy bay jumped clear, followed by two more horses. There would be another round.

The ring crew brought in a stepladder to set out the next row of bricks. The jump was raised to the very top of Mary's head. Then it went higher.

"This is nuts," Tom muttered. "It's over my head now. Mary, maybe you should pull out."

"Don't be silly," Mary laughed. She looked down at her brother, dark eyes shining. "We can do this. We can go higher. We can jump the moon!"

"What's that commotion?" Tom stretched tall, trying to see over the waiting horses to the entrance of the warm-up area, where a man was shouting.

"You have to let me in! Listen, you fool, I own one of those horses! No, I don't have a pass. Are you listening to me? That palomino mare belongs to me. I demand you let me in!"

"Oh boy," said Tom. "It's Mr. Dalton."

23

Mary stood up in the stirrups. Now she could see Simon Dalton, his face flushed with anger, arguing with the steward. "Tom, what should I do?"

"Just sit tight, Mary. Let's see what happens. I think maybe...yes, he's leaving. They didn't let him come in."

"Mr. Zee didn't tell him, did he?"

Tom shook his head, grinning. "I'm pretty sure he did not."

Mary sat down in the saddle and dismissed Simon Dalton from her mind.

Before long there was only a handful of horses and riders left outside the gate into the coliseum. Another row of bricks went up on the wall. Now it was impossible to see the horses as they approached the jump from the other side. First a pair of ears appeared, then a forelock and a head with the rider's black helmet close behind. Two bodies rising up and over.

It was the legs the audience had to watch closely. Those long, slender sticks of bone and tendon desperately folding tight in the middle at the knees, hooves tucked up close. But sometimes not tight or close enough. Just a tap from the tip of a trailing hoof was enough to send a brick tumbling to the dirt. A touch so light neither horse nor rider could feel it. The groans from the audience were the first signal they had failed.

No sighs of dismay followed Colleen's repeated attempts. Round after round she soared over the wall. As the jump grew higher, she flicked her tail in disdain after clearing it, the crowd roaring in approval.

Three riders left. Tom paced back and forth, then in circles. He marched over to the whipper-in. "How high is it now?"

"Six and a half feet," the whipper-in replied cheerfully.

Tom's hat went up and down. "Oh boy. Boy oh boy." He walked another circle.

"Ladies first," called the whipper-in, and Mary rode into the ring.

As soon as she appeared, the audience erupted in a storm of cheering and clapping. The noise abated the moment Colleen shifted into canter and began her approach to the wall. In the sudden hush, her hoof-beats could be clearly heard: one, two, three; one, two, three; up and over.

Mary pushed herself up off the mare's neck and looked back. Every brick along the top of the wall was firmly in place. She threw her arms around her horse's neck as a fresh volley of cheering rolled out of the stands.

The dark bay jumped clear but not the blaze-faced chestnut.

Two horses left. The ring crew laid down another row of bricks.

"Seven feet, sir," the whipper-in informed them.

Tom's hat came off. He held it to his chest. "Mary, this is crazy! Seven feet! It's impossible."

"It *is* possible, Tom. Don't you see? I'm riding Colleen again. *That* seemed impossible until now. Tonight's special. It's…it's magic. Can't you feel it?"

"What is going on here? Mary Inglis, why are you on that horse? Get off her right now!" Simon Dalton bellowed, stomping across the warm-up area. "Where is Zelinski?"

A steward in evening dress stepped out of the shadows, where he'd been overseeing the warm-up ring. "Sir, may I see your pass?"

"Here it is! And don't tell me it's not in order, because it was just issued!"

"Mr. Dalton, please keep your voice down. If you have a problem you must take it up with the show committee."

"I have a problem all right." He pointed at Mary. "This…girl is riding my horse without my permission. I have already spoken with the show committee. I want her off—"

"Simon, leave it alone." Charlie Peters appeared at Dalton's side.

"Peters! Where's Zelinski? Why isn't he riding the mare? What's the girl doing on her?"

Charlie took Dalton's arm and steered him to the

entrance into the ring. "Look! That's what that girl is doing—jumping your horse to a win in the Puissance!"

Dalton gaped at the height of the wall. "She'll never do it! Look at that jump. It's over six feet high."

"Seven feet exactly," said Mary.

"She'll never do it," Dalton repeated. "She shouldn't try, she's just a girl. What if she gets hurt?"

"Simon, she's gotten this far. She has a way with the mare—it's uncanny."

"Gentlemen, the next round is ready to begin," said the steward. "Will you continue or concede the competition?"

Simon Dalton crossed his arms and squinted up at Mary. She met his gaze without hesitation. He sighed and nodded. "Go on, get in there."

Mary grinned and urged Colleen into the ring.

Seven feet. *Seven feet!*

The thought jiggled into her centre of calm. She forced it aside, focused on Colleen's pace. The turn to the wall was coming up soon. Any moment now she would choose the track that would take the mare right over the middle of the jump. A quaver of anxiety: turn now or wait?

Colleen decided. She swept around the turn, picking the path she'd followed so many times already.

The wall loomed before them, a solid, wide barrier. Seven feet tall. Ridiculously high. Impossibly high. Mary felt her fingers begin to tighten, her arms start to pull back on the reins to stop Colleen. Just in time she forced her muscles to let go.

She lifted her chin high, set her line of sight higher, higher, higher. Up to the rafters, to that banner hanging there. Let Colleen choose her pace, let her pick the takeoff spot. She could do it better than any human. Just stay with her, *be* with her.

A surge forward. The mare's neck suddenly dipped low. Her forelegs buckled, then stiffened, catapulting her front end at the jump. Her hind end crouched down so low she was nearly sitting. She reared up and thrust herself into the air.

Mary's arms were straight out, reaching forward to release the reins. She felt the bump of Colleen's withers against her midsection, the rough tickle of her mane on her face. The mare's long body was stretched out in full flight over the wall. For the longest seconds of Mary's life they hovered in the wide open air.

Colleen's neck and shoulders fell away. They were descending, dropping down with surprising force. Mary's shoulders pitched forward. Instinctively, she shoved her feet out in front and struggled to pull her body back. The mare's front hooves landed and she flung up her neck, catching Mary and pushing her into the saddle.

The crowd was screaming. Mary scrabbled back into position. Colleen raced around the arena, tossing her head with pride. People were calling their names, jumping up to applaud them as they galloped by. Mary stood in her stirrups and held one hand high, two fingers spread in a victory salute. She turned Colleen into the centre of the ring and eased her to a halt. Then she saluted the audience and, finally, her beautiful, gallant mare.

The crowd went wild. The coliseum vibrated to the thunder of the applause.

"Easy, girl, it's okay. It's all for you." Mary stroked the mare's neck. Colleen was trembling, her ears flicking nervously at the volume of noise.

The clapping followed them out the gate, where the only other contestant waited to take his turn at the wall.

Mary vaulted from the saddle. Her brother wrapped her in a bear hug. "That was amazing." Then he threw his arms around Colleen and hugged her, too. The mare reached around and, grabbing his cowboy hat in her teeth, tossed it into the air.

Laughing, Tom picked up his hat, and they hurried to the gate just in time to see the dark bay make his turn to the wall and disappear from sight. The stands were eerily silent. Mary's heart thudded as several long seconds passed. Then two ears rose above the top of the wall. The dark bay sprang into view. His front legs passed over the jump, then his body and finally his hind end, twisting to clear the height.

He had nearly touched down when a sigh drifted from the stands. A single brick teetered and toppled to the ground.

The rider looked back and shook his head.

Mary stood frozen in place. Her heart thumped against her ribs. She was surrounded by people, laughing and shaking her hand and even hugging her, but everyone seemed to be far away. As if in a dream.

Was that what this was? A dream?

She felt a hand on her shoulder and turned to see Henry Zelinski smiling down at her. "Well done. *Very* well done." And then she knew it was true.

She had won.

"Come on, they want you back in the ring." Tom legged her up. Proudly, he led Colleen in at the head of a long parade of competitors.

Simon Dalton accepted the trophy with a speech, ribbons were pinned to bridles and hands were shaken. Everyone smiled for the photographs. A band marched in to play the national anthem. Mary sat tall in the saddle as she sang, one hand resting on her mare's mane, blinking away tears.

They had won.

* * *

November 22, 1955

I can't believe how everything has changed! Mr. Dalton wants me to ride Colleen from now on. He's going to pay for everything! And

Mr. Zee, well, Mr. Dalton's taken him to Ireland to look for horses. If they find one or two or three (Mr. Dalton wants to have a whole stable of winning jumpers), Mr. Dalton will buy them and fly them home. On an airplane!

Charlie Peters told Mr. Dalton he doesn't think Colleen is "reliable" enough to be on the Olympic team, even though she won the Puissance. We're going to show him! Because that's something else that has changed. Women are now allowed to jump in the Olympic Games! There's a lady rider named Pat Smythe in England. I read in a magazine that she's going to be on the British team with her horse Flanagan.

If Flanagan and Pat Smythe can do it, so can Colleen and I.

Things are changing at home, too. Miss Johnson is going to be my new mother. She and Dad are getting married. I'm really happy. She's so nice and now Dad won't be all alone when I'm off jumping in horse shows. Tom is seeing a girl in town called Debbie Rogers. His face turns beet red every time he says her name (and he says it a lot!), so I guess it's pretty serious. Maybe I'll have a new sister and a new mother.

There's lots more but I'm not feeling so good. Kind of achy and sore and really hot. My head is pounding. I must have the flu. Think I'll go to bed now. I'll write more tomorrow.

24

Faye turned to the next entry. The page was blank.

She flipped through the rest of the diary. All the pages were blank.

Faye went through the book again, slowly this time, page by page.

I'll write more tomorrow, Mary had written. But she hadn't. She hadn't written another word.

Faye closed the book in disappointment. Just when she was set to begin a new round of adventures, Mary had given up her diary.

What happened next? Faye wondered. Did Mary make it onto the team with Colleen? Did they compete in the Olympics?

Her phone buzzed in her pocket. Kirsty had sent her a text: *Get back here right away.* Faye checked the time. She'd been away from the booth for nearly three hours.

She gathered up her garbage and squeezed through the bodies in the stands to the stairs. Tossing the garbage in a can, she hurried out of the building and darted through the crowd to make her way back to the Safe Haven booth.

Kirsty was at the far end, talking to an elderly lady leaning on a cane and wearing a long, dark blue skirt. Faye gave her a quick smile. The old woman looked familiar, but Faye couldn't think of her name.

"I'm here," she puffed.

Kirsty spun around. "Finally!"

"I'm so sorry if I made you late for your barrel racing—"

"No, no, it's not that. Faye, this is Mrs. Inglis. She donated all those boxes of books, but there was one she wanted to keep."

"It's a diary. About this big." The woman rested her elbows on her cane and held up her hands to show the size. "I kept it when I was a girl. My niece helped me pack up the books and put it in the wrong box by mistake. And I'm Miss Inglis, not Mrs."

Faye stared at the black eyes glinting out from under hooded lids. The dark hair was cut off at the chin and shot through with streaks of iron grey. The years had crumpled the skin and carved out sharp cheekbones and a strong chin, but it was still the face in the photographs, Mary Inglis's face.

She looked down at the diary in her hand. "Here it is."

"Oh, good, you have it," said Kirsty. "Mom and Stuart and I looked through every box and couldn't find it."

"What were you doing with my diary?" asked Mary Inglis sharply. "Did you read it?"

Faye nodded. "I did. I'm sorry. I know I shouldn't have but—"

"That's right, you shouldn't have. That diary is my private property. Do you understand the meaning of the word 'private'?"

A middle-aged woman appeared at Miss Inglis's side. "Auntie, what's wrong?"

"This girl read my diary! My private diary!"

"Oh dear." The woman shot Faye a rueful smile. "I can see how upsetting that is for you."

"Roxanna, please don't use any of that psycho-babble nonsense with me. I may be old but I haven't lost my marbles yet."

This time Roxanna didn't bother to hide her grin. "You know, Auntie, you've had an amazing life. I don't blame this young lady for being interested in it."

"Give that to me." Mary Inglis jerked her chin at the diary.

Faye held out the book. Leaning on the cane, Mary snatched the diary away, stuffing it into the canvas bag slung across her shoulder.

Roxanna leaned across the table. "Girls, thank you for finding Aunt Mary's diary."

"If we don't get a move on, Roxanna, we're going to be late," said Mary. With her niece beside her, the old woman began to hobble off. The crowd shuffled over to fill in their empty spaces.

Faye stared after them.

"Faye, don't just stand there in everyone's way," said

Lucy, squeezing past with an armful of saddle blankets. "Do something!"

Faye ducked down. On her knees and one hand, she crawled under the table and ran into the crowd after Mary and her niece.

She caught up with them as they entered the barn area. "What happened next? I have to know. Please, tell me."

Mary didn't reply. She rapped a man's ankle with her cane. He jumped aside and she slipped through the opening he'd left. "Come on, Roxanna."

Faye followed them. Mary led the way, whacking ankles and shins with her cane to clear a path. Her lurching gait covered the ground at the pace of an able-bodied person's jog. She halted outside a box stall and swung around to glare at Faye. "Why are you following us? Who are you, anyway?"

"I'm Faye March. Maybe you know my grandmother, Lucy March?"

Mary Inglis nodded. "I've met her. I should have recognized you with all that red hair, just like your grandma's when she was a lot younger. So you're the granddaughter that's riding that rich fellow's horses—what's his name?"

"Laurence Devries," supplied Faye.

"Yes, him." The hooded lids drooped low, narrowing the black eyes to slits. "'A rising young star'—that's what they called me once. But that was a long time ago."

"Yes, I know. Please, Miss Inglis, will you tell me what happened? After the Royal Winter Fair. What happened next?"

Roxanna slipped into the box stall with a tote of brushes. "I'll get him ready for you, Auntie. Sit down and have a bit of a rest."

"Yes, thank you." Mary shuffled over to a bale of hay and lowered herself down. "Sit down. I don't like people looming over me. Now you tell me something. Why are you wearing that sling? What have you done to your arm?"

"I've sprained my shoulder. A young horse fell with me. When we were jumping."

Mary winced. "Ouch. Did that myself once. Hurts worse than a broken bone, doesn't it?"

"I've never broken anything, but this does hurt a lot."

"No broken bones, eh? Well, you've been lucky. So, do you think you'll get over it?"

"The doctor says it should heal up just fine."

"And what about you? Will you get over it?" Mary asked.

Faye hesitated. "I don't know. I can't forget Exeter falling on me. I try not to think about it, but the same scene keeps playing over and over in my head. I wish it would stop! I wish I could think of something else!"

"That's what they used to say about women riders— that we were too scared of getting hurt to be top-class competitors."

Faye hung her head in shame.

"Oh, quit feeling so sorry for yourself," said Mary briskly. She nudged Faye's ankle with her cane. "You'll be back in the ring in no time. What's that? Speak up, I can't hear you."

"I said, I don't know if I want to. I don't know if I want to jump anymore, not at horse shows. Mr. Devries expects me to win, all the time, and he's so disappointed when I don't. And Patty—that's his groom—she's always telling me I do everything wrong. I have to do my school work all by myself. I miss my friend Kirsty and my grandma and my brother. I didn't expect it to be like this. Everyone tells me this is such a great opportunity for me, but no one knows how hard it is!"

"Have you talked about this with your grandma?"

Faye shook her head. "No. I haven't told anyone. No one's going to understand. No one knows what it's like. No one but you."

"So that's what you want from me? You want me to tell you what to do."

"What *should* I do?"

"Faye, I can't make your choices for you. And that's what this is, a choice. Give up or go on."

"Is that what you did? Did you give up jumping? Is that why you stopped writing in your diary?"

Mary traced a pattern in the dirt with the tip of her cane. For a long time she didn't answer. Out of the corner of her eye, Faye studied the face of the old woman, searching for the young girl she'd once been, bright and daring and hungry for everything the world had to offer. In just a few hours she'd grown close to the young Mary, had ached for her losses and setbacks and cheered for her triumphs. She'd yearned to know her, have her as a friend, a big sister. What had the years done with that girl?

Mary heaved a long sigh and spoke. "I gave up jumping because I had no choice. I got polio."

"Oh!" Caught by surprise, Faye groped for something to say. "I...I'm sorry."

"Faye, what do you know about polio?"

"Not a lot. I know it's a really bad disease that people used to get a long time ago."

"That's right, you don't hear about it so much anymore. Thank goodness, I say. They began vaccinating for it in 1955, the same year I got it, but they started with the young children. I didn't get the vaccine in time. And you're right, it is a really bad disease. It paralyzes you. Your limbs grow weaker and weaker and eventually you can't move."

Faye reeled with the horror of it all. "But you got better, didn't you?"

"Mostly. It took a long time and a lot of hard work, and I never regained control of some of my muscles, especially on my right side. That's why I walk with this." Mary held up her cane.

"Oh, I thought you used it because you were old," blurted Faye. Her cheeks grew hot at her own tactlessness. "I'm sorry, that didn't come out right."

Mary waved away her apology. "Don't worry about it. I'm not ashamed of being old or of being disabled."

Faye fell silent, her throat tightening with sadness. She'd had her own losses—her parents, whom she missed every day; her beloved pony Robin, who now belonged to another girl. She'd connected so quickly with the young Mary Inglis and expected from the diary what she expected from any story, the comfort of a happy ending. Instead, there was this tragedy. "It's terrible that happened to you! Just when everything was going well…You never got a chance to ride in the Olympics with Colleen," she said.

"Yes," sighed Mary. "There were a lot of things I never got to do."

The stall door opened and Roxanna led out a stocky palomino gelding. "He's ready for you, Aunt Mary."

Faye recognized the palomino's snaffle bridle, but it took her a few moments to identify the strange saddle on his back. "That's a sidesaddle."

"Yes, it is. With my right side the way it is, I find it easier to ride sidesaddle," said Mary.

"You still ride!"

"I sure do." Mary pushed herself to her feet. Leaning on her cane, she stroked the horse's neck. "Meet Colin. He's Colleen's great-great-, oh, I forget how many greats, grandson."

"Colleen had foals?"

"Eight beautiful babies, one each for all my nieces and nephews and half-brothers and half-sisters."

"So Tom got married?"

Mary nodded. "To a lovely girl named Debbie. A few years before that, my father married my school-teacher, Miss Johnson. Mama Catherine we called her. She was wonderful. Oh, I might as well tell you the rest of the story."

Soon Faye learned it all—how Henry Zelinski had great success with the horses Simon Dalton brought over from Ireland and made it onto the Olympic team. How, soon after the Games were over, Mr. Dalton sold the ranch to a group of wealthy investors Charlie Peters had recruited. How Tom was appointed assistant manager and took over running the ranch when Mr. Zee retired—while Dorothy stepped into Miss Johnson's post as schoolteacher and remained there for many years.

"But what about Colleen?" asked Faye.

"Well, that's the wonderful part of the story. Just before he sold the ranch, Mr. Dalton turned up in our yard with Colleen beside him. He pulled an envelope out of his pocket and handed it to me. Inside was a bill of sale with my name down as the owner. He gave me back my Colleen." Mary sniffed. "It was one of the happiest days of my life."

"Auntie," said Roxanna, "it's time to go." She helped Mary into a dark blue jacket and passed her a helmet and a long whip.

Mary tapped the gelding's knee with her cane. The palomino folded his front legs and knelt down.

Murmuring softly to the horse, she shuffled close and lowered herself into the sidesaddle. With both hands, her whip tucked under her arm, she lifted her right leg over the fork at the top of the left saddle flap. Her left foot wiggled into the single stirrup. She tossed her cane to Roxanna. "Colin, up!"

The gelding straightened his front legs.

Sitting tall in the saddle, Mary looked down at Faye. "There you are. Now you know what happened. I've had a good run. Good family, good friends, good horses and good times. I'm a lucky woman." She scratched Colin's withers, imitating a friendly horse gesture. "You came looking for advice, so here you are. You're going to be afraid sometimes, and that's okay. Life can be scary at times. But don't be afraid of *being* afraid. Because that's what will stop you. That's the kind of fear that will keep you paralyzed."

Her black eyes held Faye's. Then she grinned, and the years fell away. There was Mary, fourteen and on top of the world, dark eyes sparkling, chin jutting out, determined to conquer all before her. Young Mary winked and gave her a nod. *You'll do okay.*

Faye closed her eyes, feeling the confusion that had tugged her here and there for weeks ebb away and a sense of certainty flow in. "Thank you," she began, opening her eyes, but Mary was gone, riding away on Colin. The old woman sat tall and proud in the saddle, her long blue skirt draped over her horse's left side.

"There are no seats left," cried Kirsty in dismay as she and Faye stood at the top of the stairs into the Agriplex.

"Faye, over here!" Roxanna waved to her from up in the stands.

"Come on, Kirsty." Faye led her friend up the stairs.

Roxanna shifted over to make room for them. "We'll have to squeeze together tight. I think every person on the grounds is here."

"Here she comes," said Faye.

A smattering of applause greeted Mary's entrance into the ring on Colin. She halted in the middle and bowed to the crowd. Lifting her head high, she waited on her golden horse. Faye shivered.

"Are you cold?" asked Kirsty.

"No. Just excited." She'd forgotten how much she loved the electric atmosphere created by a big audience.

Roxanna turned to Faye. "Thanks for talking to Auntie about the old days. Most people just think of her as that disabled woman who rides sidesaddle. They forget what a great athlete she was. And sometimes I think she does too."

Colin startled at a crackle from the loudspeakers. Mary sat him easily. Then the music began, lilting and haunting, and the palomino horse and his elderly rider began to dance.

"Beautiful," sighed Kirsty as Colin floated over the ground.

At an invisible signal from his rider, he sashayed left, then right. He marched across the arena, flinging his legs out with extravagant joy. He cantered, skipping lightly along. Then the music slowed to a strong, primeval beat. The golden horse arched his neck under his silver mane and lifted his feet high. The audience began to clap, measuring out the beats of his prancing trot. The music reached a crescendo. Colin crouched low on his hindquarters. Slowly his front end lifted, forelegs bent. Endless seconds passed as he held the pose, a rearing golden statue. He set his front feet back onto the ground and the music drifted away. Mary held up her hand in a salute to the audience. As applause echoed from the high ceiling of the building, Mary turned the horse, searching the crowd. She waved to Roxanna. Then, catching sight of Faye, she held up her index and middle fingers, split apart.

Faye lifted her hand above her head and mirrored Mary's salute.

Vee for victory.

JULIE WHITE lives on a horse
farm in Armstrong, B.C. She and her
husband, Robert, a former jockey,
raise Thoroughbreds for racing and
jumping. She rides every day and
competes in jumping classes at horse
shows, often against her two grown
daughters. She's a Pony Club
examiner, riding instructor and
course designer.

The Secret Pony
by Julie White

When they move out to the country after the divorce, Mom promises 12-year-old Kirsty a pony, but money is tight. Then Lancelot comes along, and Kirsty finds a way to buy him. He's only half trained, but he's all hers, and Kirsty is overjoyed … except for the niggling guilt about not telling her mother.

Then Kirsty falls and lands in the hospital—and in hot water. Lancelot must go! But at the last moment, Kirsty finds the support she needs, and it comes from the most unexpected source.

Our Choice Award
Chocolate Lily Award

ISBN 978-1-55039-148-0
Also available as an ebook.

High Fences
by Julie White

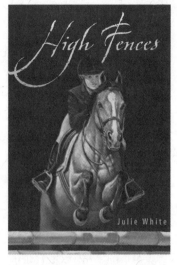

Robin is a pony in a million, and 12-year-old Faye adores him. But when her grandmother starts talking about selling the farm, Faye does the unthinkable. Heart breaking, she agrees to sell Robin.

Robin's new owner is Nicole, a spoiled rich girl with no idea how to handle him. Nicole pesters Faye to divulge her "secret" to make Robin jump. Soon there is a secret—Faye's, Nicole's and Robin's. Faye thinks she's getting what she wants and doing the best thing for Robin, too. But maybe there's a time when winning means losing the best partner you've ever had.

ISBN 978-1-55039-163-3
Also available as an ebook.

Riding Through Fire
by Julie White

Twelve-year-old Kirsty is asked to help with a cattle round-up, and she agrees, even though she's nervous. This kind of riding is completely new. Can her pony Lancelot handle it? Can Kirsty?

It's bad luck that her round-up partner is 14-year-old Jesse, who treats her like an idiot. Soon she's furious—and Jesse has disappeared. By the time she finds him, a forest fire is raging nearby. To save their lives, Kirsty and Jesse must cooperate—and trust the horse sense of the amazing Lancelot.

ISBN 978-1-55039-199-2
Also available as an ebook.

Under the Wire
by Julie White

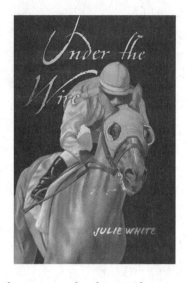

When 16-year-old Reid's jockey mother takes a fall, their horses become his responsibility. That's fine; he's always been his mother's right hand. He'll hold the fort, and when she returns he'll be back on track to his own future as a jockey.

But suddenly his best chance at the big stakes is taken away. And when his mother comes back, she drops a bomb: she's getting out of the jockey business and wants Reid to get out, too. Steaming mad, Reid takes off—but then his new friend Ella spots a big opportunity. Can Reid prove to everyone that he's got what it takes to get in first under the wire?

White's intimate familiarity with the equestrian world brings a vivid realism to her exciting horse novels.

ISBN 978-1-55039-198-5
Also available as an ebook.